THAT'S WHAT love BECOMES

Edited by Jenny Sims

Proofread by Barren Acres Editing

Cover Design by Fieriz Book Cover Design

Formatted by Kari Grindel

ISBN: 979-8-98934473-4

DEDICATION

*This dedication is for all the people who
have supported me through my life's journey.
Your unwavering love and support have been the
cornerstones of my success.*

To my mom, you understand the essence of this
book, and I love you deeply. Despite our differences,
you have always been there for me, offering the
gentle care and protection that only a mother can
give.

To dad, the one who's not blood but loves me
as his own. If it weren't for you, I wouldn't know the
sound of a father's comforting voice, always there to
guide and support.

To my brother, you and I butt heads very often,
but I love you no matter what, and we both know
what it was like back then. No one else can fully
understand the pain we've been through.

To my sister, who will never fully understand
this world. Even though you're unable to read this
book and dedication, I know you can understand my
love for you.

To my future husband, thank you for everything.
Words cannot describe how happy I am to have
such a great man in my life. You are my rock, my
soulmate. I'm glad we found each other.

CONTENT WARNINGS

Family trauma.
Will contain strong language.
Talks about grief/parent passing.
Abusive father.
Verbal / emotional abuse.
Explicit Sexual Content

THAT'S WHAT *love* BECOMES

BREWING LOVE
& LATTES SERIES

AMY ROSE

CHAPTER ONE

The wooden dock beneath me feels rough and cool where I sit, taking in the soothing waves. My hair tousles with the salty breeze, and I soak up the warmth of the midday sun.

I haven't heard from my dad in almost a year. I'd finally mustered the strength to cut him out of my life. While the decision was agonizing, I knew it was the right one. I'd been subjected to his verbal abuse for too long. The continuous flow of unkind words that diminished my self-worth was like waves crashing against the shore, wearing me down each passing day.

I noticed his behavior more after my mom remarried. One time, he took me on a field trip, and I realized he and Mom had been arguing.

Today is the day of our field trip, and my dad is joining me and my classmates to explore the fair's aquatic wonders. As we step out the front door, I notice a faint frown on his face. Last night, he and Mom had a heated argument, the details of which elude me. However, as he assists me onto the school bus, the frown dissipates, and we end up having fun. I noticed the arguing but was happy to spend time with my dad. However, as I matured into my late teens, my mom revealed she had to force him to accompany me on these field trips.

My deepest yearning has always been for an improved father-daughter relationship characterized by love, trust, and warmth. But that dream remains unfulfilled, buried under the weight of his harsh words.

Eric gazes at the expansive ocean by my side, his hazel eyes reflecting a deep understanding. Eric is the man of my dreams, who entered my life like a beacon of hope, promising love and healing.

"I wish he was a good man, Eric," I say.

His hand gently squeezes mine, and he reassures me with a soft smile. "I know. But you're strong, and you've made the right choice. You deserve love, happiness, and peace."

I return his smile, though it carries a tinge of sadness. Eric is my anchor, making me feel safe and cherished, even in the face of the darkest memories.

As the sun dips lower in the sky, I can't help but think about Scarlett's upcoming birthday. "I think it's time we plan a surprise birthday party for Scarlett, don't you?" I chirp.

"What do you have in mind?"

"She hasn't had a birthday party since her brother passed."

"What? Really?"

"Yes, they shared a birthday, one year apart."

He gives a small smile and looks back out at the ocean. "Let's head back to your house and plan it, then." He stands and extends his arm.

I grab his hand, and he lifts me to my feet. Our lips meet, and at that moment, time stands still. He pulls me closer, his touch sending shivers down my spine. The sensation of his soft, warm lips against mine ignites a fire within me, reminding me of what it feels like to truly be alive.

As I pull away, I gently intertwine our fingers, feeling the warmth of his touch.

Eric opens the fridge, taking out the thawed hamburger meat for dinner. I smile as I close the door, locking it behind me.

"Spaghetti or horseshoes tonight?" he asks.

"What are horseshoes?"

"Horseshoes is hamburger meat on top of

a slice of bread, with fries and cheese layered over it."

"That sounds good, but where did this recipe come from?"

"Springfield, Illinois. My uncle always made it when he'd come to Beaufort when I was a kid."

"All right I'll try it. I'm going to brainstorm ideas for her party," I say as I walk to him and kiss him.

"I'll let you know when it's done." I walk into my room and lie on my bed to think of ideas for her party. I grab my pen and notepad and write a list down.

- pink balloons.

- letters for happy birthday to stick to the wall.

- half chocolate/half vanilla cake with hot pink whipped icing.

I grab my cell phone and scroll through my contacts and call Scarlett's mom, Julia.

"Hello?" Julia answers.

"Hi, Julia, it's Hailey," I say cheerfully.

"Hey, girly, what's going on?"

"I was wondering if you could come to the café this Monday for Scar's birthday." I tap my pen on the paper as I wait for her answer.

"Of course! What time? I may need to call off work to head over there."

I grin before replying, "Thanks, don't tell

her, though. It's a surprise, and if you can be there by six, that'd be great."

"Sounds great. See you then."

I smile and end the call.

"Hey, beautiful, dinner is done," Eric says, walking into my bedroom.

He takes my hands and lifts me to my feet, leaning in and kissing my lips.

"Why are you so good to me?" I ask.

"Is it that hard to believe someone can be kind?" His smile is so breathtaking.

"A little."

"I love you," he says, kissing my forehead.

"I love you too."

We walk into the kitchen, and I grab a plate of food before heading toward the dining table. He's already placed a wine glass for each of us on the table, along with napkins and silverware.

"This better be tasty," I say as I take a bite.

"Oh, trust me. You'll like it."

The flavor of cheese, fries, and hamburger hits my taste buds all at once, and I widen my eyes. "Wow, this is good."

"I told you," he says.

"Wait, so you're telling me this is only in Springfield, Illinois?"

"It has spread around since it got popular,

but most people in other states don't know about it."

I take a sip of the red wine. "Well, I think we should make it a regular meal, at least in this house."

"Please do. It's one of my favorite meals."

I laugh and finish up my plate. Before I can even stand, he whisks my plate away.

"You know, I can rinse my own plate."

"Shush," he whispers and takes our dishes to the kitchen. Getting up and heading toward the living room, I plop on the couch.

"Movie night?" I yell to him in the kitchen.

"Sure."

"Could you maybe help get the balloons ready before Monday? I want to have them set up Sunday night."

"Sure. When will she be back in town?"

"Thankfully, not until Monday, so I have the advantage of being able to set things up at the café all weekend."

"You're a great friend, you know?"

I smile. "Yeah, I know." I reach for the blanket and drape it over us and turn the TV on.

Sitting here together, I think about how far we've come. He makes me feel alive, makes me feel worthy. The way his lips press against my forehead makes me feel safe.

A tear rolls down my face. My body feels calm compared to how tangled my mind is. I'm content sitting by Eric's side, but I know Ray would have loved to grill this man dating his daughter. He may have been my stepdad, but he was more of a dad than my biological one ever had been. Not a day goes by I don't miss him, and thinking about my future with Eric only makes me miss him more.

I wish I had taken the time to have more moments with Ray once I became an adult. I kind of went my own way once I moved out of my parents' house and missed out on spending time with him that I will never get back.

I haven't driven the Jeep since before he passed. As a kid, I'd sit in the driver's seat eating a bunch of french fries from my favorite fast-food place while Ray would dip his into vanilla ice cream. At the time, I thought that was disgusting, but my taste buds must have changed when I got older because it's tasty—salty and sweet. Now, it reminds me of Ray when I eat it.

Cutting my dad out means I officially have no dad in my life. Every Tuesday, I visit Ray at the cemetery. I sit on the blue throw blanket he bought me a few years ago for Christmas and just cry or laugh and tell him everything that's going on. Tuesday is a couple of days away, so it's about time to pour out my heart again. I hope he can hear me from above.

CHAPTER TWO

Sunday rolls around. Eric is out getting some groceries for tomorrow's party, so I have the place to myself.

I grab my earbuds and place them in my ears, turn on some music, and begin cleaning the house. The music doesn't drown out my thoughts, however, and I find my thoughts drifting to my dad. I wonder what I might have done wrong for my dad to be cruel.

Why doesn't he want me?

Why does he sometimes act like he wants me just to turn around and be mean again?

Did I say or do something that caused him to be such a jerk to me?

Could I have done anything differently?

All kinds of thoughts swirl in my mind. I feel they've gotten worse since I've stopped talking to him. Maybe it's the fact I know he's in jail and can't reach me. Or perhaps it's because I know I can't reach him, even if I wanted to.

But ever since I made my decision, I find myself reminiscing on my times with him, both good and bad. For years, it's been an ongoing cycle of us getting along for a few months, mostly texting, but then he blows up out of the blue, and I pause replying to him.

DAD

> Why do you never visit me?

DAD

> At least if I die, you won't have to worry about me anymore.

He's right, I wouldn't have to worry about his *bullcrap* anymore. But that doesn't mean I want him to die. He tells me lies upon lies about his health all the time.

If the blood clot situation was true, he would have had surgery, and I would've been up at the hospital for him. It's not his first round of issues with blood clots, but I also know when he's a lying asshole. If I ever get a text from him in the evening, he's drunk and talking trash. I wish he'd bother someone else sometimes.

Unfortunately, I'm an easy target for him. It's hard to explain to people why I've put up with his behavior for so long. I know why, but I'm scared to say it out loud.

If I say it out loud, it becomes real.

Healing from the pain also means truly letting him go. In my eyes, letting someone go and cutting them off are two different things. While I may have cut him off, I'm not sure I'm ready to let him go.

As I tie up the kitchen garbage bag, I notice the sky darkening. The rain starts as soon as I step outside to take out the garbage. I smile and continue getting the house in order. My mind wanders from my dad to Ray. I miss my stepdad; he was always there for me and always loved being a part of my life from the time I was a little girl.

Seven years old, I grabbed his hand and asked him if I could call him Dad, and the response he gave me when I asked him was, "You can call me anything you want." I don't recall how I replied, but he sure brought up that memory during Thanksgiving or Christmas, sometimes both every year.

I miss him so much.

I take an earbud out when I see Eric pull into the driveway. It's pouring down rain. I place the wet rag in the sink and throw my jacket on to rush outside to help him.

"Weather here is unpredictable, I swear," he grumbles while taking the bags from the car and handing some to me.

"Yeah, it's never boring here."

We hurry into the house and set the items on the counter. He puts drinks in the fridge while I grab the bag with the treats inside.

"Chocolate chip is her favorite cookie."

"Can we eat one now? Quality control and all that," he jokes.

"Sure." I open the box and hand him one. I take one and shut the box, setting it on the counter by the fridge. "No touchy till tomorrow," I singsong.

"You're silly." He laughs.

I shrug and wrap my arms around his neck. He lifts me into his arms, and I wrap my legs around his waist, kissing him. I can't believe it's been nearly a year since we began dating. I was hesitant at first because love was scary for me, and I didn't know how to trust.

Hours go by, and I sit here on the couch as Eric snoozes next to me. The thunder roars furiously outside with the pouring rain. My phone dings, and I unlock it to find a text from Scarlett.

SCARLETT

> Hey, sweet cheeks! My flight has been delayed for a few hours because of the storm. I may not be home until Monday evening.

Well, that's good. Gives me time to make sure her surprise party is ready without her being nosy! I tap a reply and hit send.

ME

That's okay, how's Florida?

SCARLETT

Florida is amazing! How's everything on your end?

I quickly type a response.

ME

Oh, just the usual chaos.

She replies with a laughing and heart emoji, and I smile. I place my phone back down and snuggle into Eric's arms, falling asleep to the beat of his heart.

Eric's phone unleashes a cacophony of electronic beeps, jolting me awake from the warmth of my cozy cocoon. In the dim glow of predawn, I groggily sit up, squinting at the bluish glare of my clock, only to be greeted by the ungodly hour of not even six o'clock.

Suppressing a yawn, I turn my gaze toward Eric, who is nestled in the clutches of deep slumber, blissfully ignorant of the morning madness. I nudge him gently, hoping not to startle him from his dreams. His eyes flutter open, resembling a bewildered owl caught mid-nap.

"You know," I say with a playful grin, "it might be time for you and your alarm clock to introduce yourselves."

Eric blinks a few times, attempting to shake off the remnants of sleep. A sheepish grin spreads across his face as he rubs his eyes, trying to grasp the reality of the waking world.

"Morning already?" he mumbles, his raspy voice a mix of confusion and reluctance.

I chuckle. "Indeed, and it seems your alarm clock and you need to establish better communication. It's been trying to reach out, but you keep ignoring it."

Eric chuckles. "Well, I'm sure its feelings aren't hurt."

"Well," I tease, "it's never too late for a proper introduction. Your alarm clock might appreciate it." I raise my brows. "I know I will."

"Oh shush." He laughs.

As we both share a laugh, he leans up and kisses me. "I have to get dressed for work."

"But do you have to?" I pout playfully, giving him my best puppy-dog eyes. He chuckles, glancing back at me with a smirk. "I wish I could stay, but duty calls," he says, caressing my cheek.

I sigh dramatically, still keeping up the pout. "Fine, but only if you bring me a coffee. And maybe a croissant from the kitchen."

He grins. "Deal. Consider it our breakfast date. Now, let me get dressed before I'm late for real."

He quickly gets dressed and heads to the kitchen. He walks back in, bringing me a coffee and my croissant.

"Thank you," I say as he kisses my forehead.

"Love you. See you after I get off work."

"I love you too."

CHAPTER THREE

I push open the door to the café. As the bell chimes above me, I take a deep breath, inhaling the comforting scent that has never failed to soothe my nerves.

The café is relatively quiet, the morning sun casting a warm glow through the windows. I can't help but smile because today is all about Scarlett. I have big plans for her surprise birthday party, and it is my job to make sure everything is perfect.

Moving with purpose, I grab a handful of menus and begin arranging the tables near the window. Scarlett loves that spot—the natural light and coziness are her favorite. I can't wait to see the look on her face when she walks in tonight.

As I wipe down the counter, my mind wanders to my stepdad, a twinge of sadness gripping my heart. It's been almost a year since he left us, and the ache of his absence lingers. He made any occasion feel special, and I can't shake the feeling he would have loved to be here, helping me set up for Scarlett's big night.

I glance at the empty chair—his favorite chair—near the entrance, a pang of nostalgia hitting me. I remember his laughter and how he teased Scarlett about her love for caffeine. Shaking my head, I try to dispel the melancholy that threatens to overshadow the joyous occasion.

As I arrange the balloons, memories of past birthdays flood my mind, reminding me of the joy and laughter that filled this space. I can't help but feel a bittersweet ache in my heart, longing for those moments to be shared once again.

With a sigh, I focus on the task at hand. I adjust the chairs, ensuring they're perfectly aligned. The streamers and balloons are ready to go, and I can't wait to surprise Scarlett with the elaborate game night I have planned—just the way she likes it.

I will make this night unforgettable, a tribute to the memories we cherish and the ones we hold close in our hearts.

Just as I step back to admire the café's transformation, my phone buzzes in my pocket, jolting me back to the present. I fish it out, the screen illuminating with Scarlett's mom, Julia, calling.

"Hey, Julia," I answer, a smile tugging at my lips. "How's it going?"

"Hailey, dear! I just wanted to let you know I'll be bringing a home-cooked meal for Scarlett's birthday. A little something to make her day extra special." Julia's warm voice crackles through the phone.

My heart swells with gratitude. Julia is like a second mom to me, always ready to lend a helping hand and spread a little extra love. "That's so sweet of you, Julia. Scarlett will be over the moon."

"Well, it's the least I can do. I'll be at the café before five thirty. I can't wait to see the look on her face!" Julia chuckles, and I can practically see her infectious smile through the phone.

"Perfect timing! We aim to start the surprise soon after. Your home-cooked touch will be the icing on the cake, so to speak."

"Great! I'll make sure it's something special. See you at five, dear."

As I hang up, I let out a heavy sigh. Julia's gesture adds an extra layer of warmth to the celebration. Scarlett's in for a treat, not just with the party but also with the homemade feast her mom is preparing.

I suck in a deep breath after I turn the café lights off. Even though it's not the holidays, these Christmas lights are perfect for her birthday. I take a seat to admire my work.

I haven't dedicated this much time to do something this thoughtful in a long time. Hell, I don't even remember the last time I did something like this. After checking the time, I look outside the back window and see her mom's blue sedan pulling into the parking lot. I rush toward the door and walk outside to help her.

"Hi, Julia, let me grab that for you," I say as I open the back door.

"Thank you, sweet girl. What time do you think she'll be here?"

"She said she'd meet me here after six thirty." I grab the Crock-Pot from the back seat. "This roast smells good," I say, closing the door with my hip.

"Thank you. It's one of Scarlett's favorites."

We walk inside, and I set the Crock-Pot on top of the counter, plugging it in.

"I'm so glad you set this up for her," she says, hands clasping together while leaning on the counter.

"She deserves it."

The bell of the front door chimes, and I look over to see Eric and my mom walking inside with pink-wrapped presents.

I smile and sprint toward Eric, giving him a big hug after he sets the gifts down.

"Hi, I missed you all day." I squeeze him in a tight hug, wrapping my arms around his neck.

"I've missed you too." His arms wrap around my waist as I breathe in his cologne.

Letting go, I look at my mom and hug her.

"Scarlett's lucky to have you," she says.

As I bite my lip, my heart pings with a slight heaviness. "I hope she loves this party. She hasn't had one since her brother passed."

"Oh, sweetie, has it really been so long? She will love that you did this for her."

I nod and wipe the tear rolling down my cheek.

"Julia, cake's in the fridge," I say.

"On it."

People arrive for the party, but it's not even six yet. Eric and I finish making the gifts look pretty, and I walk over to the tables, counting every board game to be sure it's all equal.

As everyone settles into their seats, I grab a card and hold it up. "Thank you, everyone, for coming out tonight. Game night is a special night we love to have with the community. You may notice gifts on the table and a beautiful smell of roast in the Crock-Pot over there on the counter. As some of you know, tonight is Scarlett's twenty-sixth birthday, and she will be here in about..." I check the time on my phone. "Twenty minutes. Gather your drinks, and let's settle down before she gets here. She doesn't know tonight's game night is also her surprise party. When she gets close, we'll turn the lights down and yell happy birthday when she walks in!"

Everyone gets up and heads toward the counter to grab a drink, and I see Eric walking toward me. He's so handsome. I wish I knew how I got lucky to get someone like him.

"It's been a year since we met, you know?" he says.

I nod, maintaining eye contact.

"I have a surprise back home for you," he beams.

"Oh yeah? What's that?"

"Well, if I tell you, it wouldn't be a surprise."

I smile and roll my eyes. "Okay, you tease." I lean in and give him a kiss. His soft lips pressing against mine calm every inch of my body.

"I love you," he says.

"I love you too."

My phone vibrates, and I look to see a text from Scarlett.

SCARLETT

Hey, I'm on my way. See you soon! Xx

"She's on the way. Turn the lights down and stay quiet!" I holler.

Everyone sits in their seats. I grab Eric's hand, and we waltz our way toward the front. It feels like forever, but finally, I see her car's headlights shine into the window. She gets out of the car and closes the door, then walks toward the front door.

The bells chime, and just as the door closes, Eric flicks the lights on.

"Happy birthday, Scarlett!" the entire café yells.

She cups her hands over her mouth and widens her eyes. She looks straight at me, then Eric, and scans over everyone, and eventually lands on her mom. She shrieks, "Oh my gosh, you guys!" She walks over to me, embracing me.

"I love you, bestie."

"I love you too." I look into her eyes and notice the tears trying to escape. I grab a napkin nearby and hand it to her.

"Thank you."

"Can't ruin the mascara on your birthday."

"Damn right," she says, turning around and looking at the crowd of people.

"Game night or surprise party?" she jokes.

"You know which," I say.

"Ah, that's why everyone is here." She lets out a laugh.

"Oh, come on, you've been part of our

community since we were kids, game night or not. We love you!" Chance shouts out, a guy who lived down the block from me as a kid for years.

"Well, let's get started. Y'all know the drill. Pick the first game on your table and play!" Scarlett says, and everyone begins.

The aroma of Julia's perfectly roasted dinner fills the air. My fingers trace the edge of the wine glass.

"Hailey, pass me the salad, will you?" Eric's gentle and familiar voice draws me back into the moment. The clinking of cutlery and the hum of conversation float around the room.

With a soft smile, I hand it to him, my eyes wandering around the table. Scarlett sits across from me; her mom, Julia, who has outdone herself with the roast, is next to her; and my mom beams with approval next to me.

"So, Scarlett, spill the details. How was the business retreat?"

Scarlett's gaze lifts from her plate, meeting mine with a twinkle. "It was great, Hailey. But you know, I missed the café. Missed you."

A grin tugs at the corners of my lips. "Aw, you missed my excellent coffee-making skills, didn't you?"

She laughs. "Absolutely. No one brews a latte like you do."

With a teasing glint in my eye, I probe further, "And what about meeting a handsome stranger amid all those business talks?"

A playful denial dances on Scarlett's lips. "Nope, no handsome strangers for me."

I raise an eyebrow, exchanging glances with Eric and our moms.

"Okay, whatever you say." My lips curve up.

The flickering candlelight highlights Scarlett's eyes as they shift, momentarily clouded with gratitude and sorrow. She takes a moment, a gentle inhale, before speaking. "Thank you all for making this birthday so special. It means the world to me, truly."

Our eyes meet, and I sense the weight of unspoken emotions that linger beneath her smile. The room falls into a hushed stillness, a collective acknowledgment of the absence that looms over Scarlett's heart. She traces the rim of her wineglass, lost in a moment of reflection.

"And to you, Sam. Today, we would have been celebrating your birthday too," she whispers, raising her glass slightly. The atmosphere tightens with a shared sentiment, a collective remembrance of her brother. His absence is a void we all feel keenly, the love for him binding us together.

Julia's hand finds Scarlett's across the table, a silent assurance that speaks volumes. My heart clenches at the ache in Scarlett's eyes as memories of her brother dance like shadows created by the candlelight.

"Cheers to Sam," Eric says, breaking the somber silence. We raise our glasses in unison, the clink echoing through the room. The resonance holds a melody of both joy and melancholy.

Later, as everyone in the café gathers around the cake adorned with flickering candles, Scarlett takes a deep breath before making her wish.

"Happy birthday, Scarlett," I whisper. The room erupts in applause as Scarlett blows out the candles.

CHAPTER FOUR

When Eric and I step through the front door of my house, a peculiar sight greets us. My eyes widen at the trail of delicate rose petals strewn along the hallway, leading us farther into my home. The soft light from faux candles flickers on the kitchen counter, casting a warm glow across the room.

"Oh, Eric," I exclaim. My eyes widen, my heart races, and a rush of adrenaline tingles through my body. I feel the blood rushing to my face as he takes my hand, leading me along the petal-strewn path.

The hallway leads us to my bedroom, where the soft light accents the petals scattered across the bed. "What's all this?" I ask, my words barely audible.

"Your surprise," he replies, grabbing my hands and pulling me to sit on the bed. "I want us to go on vacation somewhere across the ocean. A place you've wanted to visit for a long time."

By the look on his handsome face, I sense there's more to come. "Hawaii?" I ask.

He nods and reaches into his pocket, pulling out two plane tickets. "Oh my God!" I exclaim, grabbing the tickets and examining them. "When do we go?"

"Two weeks from today," he says. I jump to my feet, taking his hands as he stands and wraps his arm around me. "Thank you. I can't wait to tell Scar!"

"She already knows. How do you think I found out about your dream vacation?"

I squeal. "Okay, okay. Can you please run me a bath while I call her?"

"Yes, I will."

I kiss him, then head to the kitchen, grabbing a glass of wine as I tap the call button on Scarlett's name.

"Hello?"

"Girl, he's taking me to Hawaii!" I yell into the phone.

"I'm so happy for you, Hails! He's such a good guy!"

"He mentioned you helped him pick out the vacation spot."

"I did. He called me a couple of months after Christmas, and we got it set up within a week," she says.

"Where the heck was I during the

planning?" I ask.

"Working, mostly."

"Ah, so that's why I ended up with extra shifts."

"Yup, but hey, it paid off."

"Sure did! I'm headed into the bath. See you at work tomorrow," I say.

"Bye! Love ya!"

I hang up, place my phone on the counter, and head toward the bathroom. The tub is already filled with water, and I strip before stepping in. I shift my hair onto my right shoulder as I lie back into the warm water. My lips part slightly from the relaxing sensation, and I take a deep breath. Letting it go, I repeat that a few times as I close my eyes and relax.

The upcoming trip to Hawaii fills my mind with excitement and a touch of nervous anticipation. Lost in thought, I wonder if this tropical paradise might be the backdrop for a significant moment—perhaps a proposal from Eric. The idea sends a thrilling shiver down my spine as I stare off into the water, contemplating the possibilities.

A soft knock on the bathroom door jolts me back to the present, and Eric's voice follows. "Everything okay in there? Need anything?"

I smile and ask, "Want to share this tub with me?"

Eric grins. "You don't need to ask me twice."

He joins me, and soon we're both submerged in the soothing warmth of the water.

"So what's your mom like?" I inquire, genuinely interested.

Eric chuckles. "Oh, my mom, Danielle, she's a character. Huge romance book fanatic. She shelves every book she buys, whether she reads it. I once teased her that her bookshelf might reach the clouds one day."

I laugh, imagining the towering bookshelves filled with love stories. "I'd love to meet her," I say, picturing the shared camaraderie over a mutual love for romance.

"Soon, I promise. She'll love you." He pauses for a moment. "You know," he says with a warm smile, "Hawaii is just the beginning of our adventures together."

I respond, equally heartfelt, "I can't wait for all the moments we'll share." Our lips meet in a lingering kiss.

The following morning, a fast pulse runs through my body as I walk into the café, ready to begin my shift. I find Scarlett behind the counter, tying her apron on.

"Morning, Hails! Ready for another day of caffeinated adventures?" Scarlett grins, her enthusiasm contagious.

"Absolutely," I reply, mirroring her smile. "Speaking of adventures, I can't stop thinking about Hawaii. It still feels like a dream."

"Girl, you better believe it's real. Eric is quite the romantic, isn't he?"

I nod with a smile on my face. As we stock the coffee filters to prepare for the day ahead, Scarlett leans in. "Any chance you think Eric might pop the question in Hawaii?"

I raise an eyebrow, taken aback by the suggestion. "What? No way! We've only been together for a year. I doubt he's thinking about marriage already."

Scarlett smirks, teasing, "Well, you never know. He did plan this dream trip of yours, and you've been talking about Hawaii for ages. It's like a fairy-tale setting, don't you think?"

I shake my head, dismissing the idea. "Come on, Scar. Proposing? That's a bit too soon, don't you think?"

She raises an eyebrow. "Hails, when a guy takes you on your dream trip, he likely has something special up his sleeve. I've seen enough romantic movies to know."

I chuckle nervously. I don't know about that. Let's not jump to conclusions."

Scarlett winks, her smile knowing. "Well, just enjoy the ride. Who knows? Maybe your dream trip will turn into a dream proposal."

I laugh and shake my head, trying not to

get my hopes up.

Scarlett's words about a potential proposal linger in my mind as I take orders and serve coffee to the customers. I know it crossed my mind last night in the tub, but for someone else to be thinking of it makes it feel more possible. The café buzzes with the usual energy, but my mind is preoccupied with the thought of what surprises Hawaii might hold.

The scent of freshly ground beans fills the air as I find myself lost in memories of my stepdad, the man who filled the role of a father in my life. The ache in my chest intensifies as I think about the upcoming possibility of a proposal, a moment that, in my ideal world, would involve the man who was supposed to walk me down the aisle. How could I ever have a wedding without him? The question weighs heavily on my heart as I navigate the busy café, putting on a smile for the customers while grappling with the absence of a loved one who has played such a significant role in my life. He was the one who helped me with my homework and who always had a kind word and a warm hug when I needed it most. He was my rock.

As I pour steaming hot coffee into a cup, I catch my reflection in the polished surface of the espresso machine. There's a mix of emotions in my eyes—anticipation for the trip to Hawaii, excitement for the possibilities with Eric, but also a twinge of sadness, a longing for the man who won't be there to witness these milestones.

The customers' voices fade into the background as I get lost in my thoughts, grappling with the bittersweet reality of life's journey. I take a deep breath, trying to shake off the melancholy that threatens to overshadow the joy of the present moment. It's a delicate dance, balancing the weight of loss with the hope of new beginnings.

I feel a tap on my shoulder and turn around. Scarlett's eyes widen as she slightly nudges her head toward the entrance. I look and notice a delivery man holding a white envelope.

"Hi, is there a Hailey Scott here?"

I walk up to the tall man.

"That's me," I say.

He hands me the envelope and wishes me a good day.

I raise a brow, dumbfounded. I watch as he walks back to his mail truck. Scarlett walks in front of me, her head facing the window, before turning to face me.

"That was odd," she says.

I look down, and my heart drops to the pit of my stomach when I see my dad's handwriting. My biological dad. We have the same handwriting, so I recognize it immediately. Without opening it, I throw it into the nearest garbage can and take a deep breath.

"Hails, do you need a day?" she asks.

"No, I just, uh... Need to keep myself busy." I grab the coffeepot and walk around the dining area to check if anyone needs a refill.

I keep myself busy to distract my mind from the envelope. Just a few more hours and I can go home.

CHAPTER FIVE

As I sit on my couch, I think about how every accomplishment I've ever made has never felt satisfying, like I'm unworthy of any success or good in my life. I'll set goals and turn myself inside out to make them happen. I'll pat myself on the back, give myself a good pep talk, but after a while, the accomplishment doesn't feel so shiny or special anymore. We are our own worst enemy.

I tie up the garbage from the kitchen and toss it into the outside trash can and walk back inside. I look at the pile of dishes. Why can't I just do them? I don't expect anyone else but me to handle cleaning my house. Whenever Eric is about to take care of the dishes, I tell him no and that I will get to them. *But I never do.* My mind screams at me to get moving, but my body is paralyzed at having more than one task to do. Things get left out or neglected until I've been able to break through my thoughts.

I scroll through my messages, finding

Scarlett's name.

Me: *Hey, movie night?*

I walk over to the couch and sit. While waiting for her to reply, I tap the call button for Mom, placing it on speaker.

"Hi, Hails!" she says.

"Hi, Mom, what are you doing?" I say, lying back on the couch.

"I'm sitting here watching an old movie. What's going on?"

"Nothing. Just missing Dad."

I hear shuffling on the other end.

"Me too, sweetie."

"That gray long-sleeve shirt of his, is it still in the closet?"

"Yes, did you want it?"

"Yeah."

"You used to wear that all the time as a kid."

I let out a laugh. "Yeah, I remember not letting him have it back for weeks."

"You were stubborn, but he loved you so much."

My phone pings, and I look at my screen to see a text.

SCARLETT

Want me to bring pizza?

I swiftly text her back.

ME

> Yes! Save me from having to do more dishes. LOL.

I place the phone back to my ear. "Before I forget, I was calling to see if you want to go to the cemetery with me?"

"Yes, what time?"

"I can come get you after work."

"Sounds like a plan!"

"I'll let you get back to your movie, Mom. Love you."

I hang up and place my phone down, falling into a nap while I wait for Scarlett.

A knock on the door jolts me awake from my nap. I stand from the couch and head toward the front door and open it.

"Special delivery," Scarlett says with a grin, holding a pizza in one hand and soda in the other.

"Come in." I laugh.

She walks in, and I close the door. I follow

her to the kitchen, and she sets the pizza and soda on the counter.

Her eyes widen when she looks at the dirty dishes in the sink.

"Honey, are you okay?

"Unfortunately, no."

"I really think you should seek help. I know you don't enjoy going to the doctor, but you are too important to me not to bring it up."

"I know you're just trying to help, but I don't see how medicine will help me do my dishes."

"I said nothing about medicine. Talking to someone may also help you declutter that mind of yours. And don't discount the medication. There are lots of people out there with ADHD who find success with medicine. It helps quiet down their mind, helping them focus on tasks better."

"We'll see," I say, and open the cabinet only to see nothing there. I turn back around and look at the dishes. Ignoring them, I grab the pizza box and soda and sit on the couch.

I stuff my face with pizza before hearing water running in the kitchen.

"Are you seriously doing the dishes right now?" I ask with a mouth full.

"Yup!" she hollers back.

I purse my lips, eye my pizza, and set it back

in the box. I can't keep doing this to myself, but how am I supposed to fucking do something about it if I can't even get up to wash a plate or two?

My mind is in shambles.

Running water and clinking dishes continue in the background as Scarlett takes charge of the neglected kitchen. I watch her from the couch, feeling a mix of gratitude and guilt. Gratitude for having such a caring friend and guilt for not being able to handle simple tasks on my own.

Scarlett glances over her shoulder and catches my gaze. "Seriously, Hails, you need to talk to someone about this. It's not just about the dishes. I've seen you struggle with this for a while now."

I sigh, feeling the weight of her words. "I know, Scarlett. It's just hard. I feel like I should be able to handle my life without needing to rely on someone else or professional help."

She dries her hands on a towel and walks over to the couch, sitting beside me. "Hailey, asking for help doesn't mean you're weak. It takes strength to recognize when you need support. And trust me, you're not alone in this. I'm here for you, but sometimes you might need more than a friend."

I nod. I take a deep breath, my mind still a whirlwind of thoughts. "Maybe you're right. I'll consider it."

Scarlett smiles and pats my back. "Good. Now, let's enjoy this pizza and forget about the dishes and your chaotic thoughts for a while."

If only it were that easy.

As the night progresses, Scarlett heads to the kitchen to get more napkins, leaving me alone with my thoughts. The mention of my stepdad earlier in the day resurfaces, and I find myself lost in memories of him. The ache of missing him never quite fades.

She returns, handing me a napkin. "You okay?" she asks.

"Yeah, just missing my stepdad a lot today," I admit, taking a sip of the soda.

"I get it. Grief is tough, and it hits you when you least expect it. Talking about him helps, though."

"I just want to watch this movie."

As the night winds down, she glances at the clock. "I should probably head home. You sure you're okay?"

I nod with a smile.

"Yeah, thanks for everything. And thanks for the reality check about seeking help. I'll think about it, I promise."

She hugs me tightly. "You're my best friend. I'm always here for you. You're not alone in this. Remember that."

The living room is bathed in the soft

glow of the TV, the remnants of the evening scattered around—an empty pizza box with napkins inside, a large, half-empty soda bottle, and the faint scent of tomato sauce lingers in the air.

Feeling the day's exhaustion, I stretch out on the couch, my eyelids heavy. The gentle hum of the TV becomes a lullaby, and I fall asleep.

The front door creaking open rouses me from my slumber. Blinking away the remnants of sleep, I see Eric entering the house, his tired eyes meeting mine.

"Hey," he whispers.

I sit up, rubbing my eyes. "Hey."

Shrugging off his coat, he asks, "What happened here? It looks like a pizza party."

I giggle, feeling a weight lift off my shoulders with his presence. "More like a therapy session with Scarlett. She brought pizza and a reality check."

Eric raises an eyebrow. "Reality check?"

"She really suggests I see someone about my ADHD...and probably other stuff too."

His expression softens, and he sits beside me, wrapping an arm around my shoulders.

"Maybe she's onto something," he breathes. "You've been carrying a lot on your own, Hails. It's okay to ask for help."

I rest my head on his shoulder. "I know. It's just hard admitting I can't do it all by myself."

"You don't have to," he reassures me. "We're a team, remember?"

His words sink in, and I smile, grateful for the unwavering support. "Yeah, we are."

He presses a kiss on my forehead. The weight of the world feels a little lighter with him by my side.

"Let's clean up this mess tomorrow," Eric suggests. "Tonight, let's just relax."

CHAPTER SIX

"SCARLETT, HAND ME THAT RAG, PLEASE?" I LET OUT A sigh. My day has been shit. Some customers have been very bitchy today, making me want to throw coffee at the wall. The amount of frustration I've developed today because of their attitudes has made me spill coffee on myself more than once.

"Stop being so clumsy," she says as she hands me a rag.

"I can't help it. I'm shaking so bad I just want to sit."

"Then sit. When you first started here, I told you to take a break when you feel overwhelmed."

"I feel bad. We have so many customers today. I just don't want to do that to you."

She grabs my shoulders and slightly pushes me to sit on a chair at the counter. "Honey, I can handle it. Just sit."

"Okay." I wipe the coffee grounds from my

jeans and set the rag down on the counter in front of me. Today is not my day. I look at the time on my phone; it's thirty minutes before I have to pick up Mom and head to the cemetery. Sometimes it feels like time slows right before I'm about to clock out.

As I scroll through my social feed on my phone, my mind wanders to the letter I received from my dad. Why would he have one sent to me at work? I don't get it. Probably just another of his manipulation tactics.

For years, I've struggled to love myself because of the cruel things he'd said to me. I still don't understand why I didn't cut him out of my life sooner.

My phone pings, and I look up to see a text from Mom.

Mom

Hey, sweetie, I have a terrible cough coming on. I don't want you to get sick. I will visit the cemetery with you next Tuesday.

Pressing my lips slightly, I hover my thumbs over the keyboard and type a reply.

ME

> It's okay, love you. I'll drop off some food for you when I am done.

I put my phone in my front pocket and get back to work.

It's been about twenty minutes now since I parked the car. The cemetery awaits me, but I can't seem to get out of the car. Sometimes I wonder if Ray can actually hear me when I talk to him.

I sigh, grabbing my blanket, and open the car door. I slowly walk toward his gravesite. I drape my blanket over the freshly mowed grass and sit down.

"I miss you, Ray," I say. The birds chirp in the tree next to me, their sounds bringing a sense of calmness. I take a shaky breath, my chin quivers, and I swallow back the tears.

"It's been almost a year since I cut you-know-who out of my life, and I'm sure you'd be proud of me putting myself first."

A tear rolls down my cheek, and I can't contain them anymore. My throat aches as I cry out as silently as I can to avoid someone hearing me. "I'm so sorry for not seeing you more often after I moved out. My depression got the best of me, and leaving my house was too much."

I pause, taking a breath.

"I love you, Mom loves you, Scar misses you. I miss you. Everyone hates you are gone." I wipe the tears off my face, but it's useless. More tears fall, and I pull the collar of my shirt up and just cry into it, allowing the cotton to soak up the continuous tears.

The breeze carries my whispered words as I sit here, my emotions lying bare in Ray's resting place. As I compose myself, I glance at the tombstone, tracing the engraved letters with my fingertips. It's beginning to darken out here, the sun casting long shadows over the cemetery. I take a deep breath, trying to steady my emotions. The approaching anniversary of Ray's passing brings an extra touch of sadness.

Time keeps moving, marking both the good and tough moments. Visiting the cemetery has become a routine, a way to connect the present reality with the past I can't let go of.

I stand and grab my blanket. "I'll see you next week, Ray," I say and walk back to my car.

Entering the house, Eric wraps his arms around me like a warm blanket. His eyes meet mine; he knows this time every Tuesday is when I come home with a tearstained face. He moves closer, cupping my face, and the world around me fades.

As our lips meet, my tense shoulders relax. He pulls away and hugs me tighter. "I bought pizza," he says.

"Pepperoni?" I ask.

"You know it," he whispers in my ear.

He pulls away, kissing me on the cheek, and walks to the kitchen.

"Not sure if you noticed, but the dishes are done," I say.

He looks at the sink and looks at me. "Scarlett?" he asks.

I nod. "I think it's time I seek professional help."

"Did you want to call your doctor this week to schedule something?"

"Yeah, I'll do it tomorrow." Crossing my arms, I walk over to him and give him a kiss. "I don't want to talk much about it until after our vacation."

"Okay, well, let's head out to the beach. Spend some time together outside of the house."

"Sounds good. Let me grab my phone."

I roll the window down just as he pulls out onto the street. The warm Carolina breeze blows through my hair and hits my face. I've only ever lived on the Atlantic Ocean. I wonder if the water feels different in Hawaii.

"You're so beautiful," he says.

Heat travels to my face. "Oh, stop."

"What? You are."

He interlocks our fingers, then brings my hand to his face and kisses it.

I place my hand behind his neck, playing with the ends of his hair. I could sit here forever as long as I'm with him.

The beach comes into view, and he pulls into the parking lot.

"Stay here."

"What? Why?" I ask.

"Because I have a surprise for you. So wait for me."

I arch my eyebrows. "Another surprise? All right, I'll wait here."

He gets out of the car and walks out toward the sand, and because of a tree being in the way, I can barely see him. What is he up to? After a few minutes, I see him walking back to my side of the car and opening the door. "Come on," he says, reaching out his hand. I grab it and climb out of the car. "Close your eyes."

I giggle. "I may fall, though."

"I'm right here if you do."

"Promise?"

"I promise."

I close my eyes, and he guides me wherever he takes me. "You know, this is how some people die."

"Oh shush, you're fine."

"Says the one without their eyes covered."

He chuckles, and we stop. "Open."

I do as he says and gasp, placing my hand over my chest as my heart bangs against it. On the sand right in front of the ocean water lays a big soft red blanket with a pizza box and a wine bottle.

"Oh, this is so cute! I love it!" I turn around, my heart fluttering like a trapped bird in my chest. His eyes meet mine, and I feel a surge of warmth and longing deep within me as if every cell in my body reaches out for him. He inches closer to me, gazing down at my lips before looking back into my eyes. At this moment, I can't help but wonder if he feels the same intense desire as I feel coursing through my veins and knows how much I crave his touch. As his hand gently glides across the back of my neck, pulling me into a kiss, goosebumps spread through my body, electrifying every nerve ending. I can feel the heat of his palm against my skin, sending a rush of warmth and anticipation through my entire body. The kiss deepens, and our tongues entwine. I caress his forearm, his hands on my hips.

"I want you now," I say between kisses, my voice filled with longing and urgency.

The words escape my lips with a raw honesty that surprises even me.

"Publicly?"

"Yeah." My heart pounds as I speak.

"You're lucky it's dark, and no one's here," he murmurs, his voice laced with desire and a hint of mischief. The words hang in the air, teasing me with the forbidden thrill.

The sun has set, and the moon casts a soft glow on our surroundings.

He removes his shirt, his movements deliberate and unhurried, as if savoring every moment leading up to this. Teasing me, he traces delicate patterns near the edge of my shirt with his fingers. The playful glint in his eyes matches the butterflies fluttering in my stomach.

He lays me down on the blanket, his touch gentle and reverent, like he's holding something fragile and precious. Fumbling with the buttons of my jeans, he trembles slightly, betraying his own excitement and nervousness. His touch is hesitant and eager, a delicate balance between restraint and unrestrained passion.

My eyes linger on his muscles, the sight of his sculpted physique igniting a fire within me.

His cologne's rugged and masculine scent fills the air, mingling with the earthy aroma of the surroundings.

I moan as his lips trail kisses along my inner thigh, a small whimper escaping my parted lips. Every touch, every sensation, sends waves of pleasure coursing through me, making it hard to focus on anything else.

As his warm breath caresses my skin, I can't help but surrender to the vulnerability that washes over me. At this moment, I am completely exposed, my desires laid bare before him, and it both terrifies and exhilarates me.

The warmth of his tongue against my throbbing clit sends a surge of electricity through my body as if every nerve ending is on fire. Pleasure and desire swirl within me, overwhelming my senses and blurring the line between reality and ecstasy.

His fingers trace a delicate path along my skin, a touch that speaks volumes of his desire to please and protect.

"Please, I need you," I say as I look down at him. He nods, but instead of going all in, he flicks his tongue slowly.

"Eric, if you don't make me come right now, I swear..." My voice is laced with frustration and need. His hands hold my hips, not just with desire, but with a tender grasp that makes me feel safe and exposed all at once. He licks deeper and faster, igniting a wildfire of pleasure that consumes my body.

My back arches involuntarily as his tongue dances expertly, with every touch electrifying and sending waves of ecstasy through me. As he pulls me more into his mouth, I can feel the wet heat enveloping me, intensifying the pulsating ache between my thighs.

When I come undone, I'm so glad to be able to call this man mine.

CHAPTER SEVEN

As the week goes by, my excitement for Hawaii increases. I lean forward, resting my elbows on the counter. Rush hour. The busiest time of the day is about to start. Everyone on the block comes in to get something to eat with a coffee, sometimes even a juice or soda. A line begins to form, and the first customer walks up to the counter. "Hi, is this to go, or would you like to dine in?" I ask.

"I'd like to dine in."

"Sure, follow me." I grab a menu and walk the customer to her seat. "What can I get started for you?" I ask.

"I'll just take a mocha frappé and the house salad."

"Anything else?" I say as I write down her order.

"No, thank you."

"All right, Scarlett or I will be back with your order."

"Thank you!"

"You're welcome."

I walk back to the counter and get the other customers taken care of.

Everyone seems to be in a good mood today, which is great because I don't need my mood dragged down. As I count inventory, I think about Mom. Oh crap, I forgot to take her food after the cemetery.

"Hails, do you think you and Eric could host game night on Friday?" Scarlett asks.

"Yeah, are you going somewhere else?"

"I have a date."

"Oh yay! With who?"

"Zack."

He moved, but rumor has it he's coming back home. She has a big heart, and he better not break it.

"Are you two officially together?"

"After tonight, I hope so."

"He seems like a nice guy, but be careful. Remember when that one girl tried to fight you because of him?"

"Yeah, well, she's a bitch, and that's probably why he's not with her anymore."

I laugh. "You're probably right."

"Besides, he is a nice guy,"

"Better be. Otherwise, he's gonna have to

sleep with one eye open."

"Put them claws away, Hails! I appreciate it, though."

"Hey, gotta protect my girl!"

"Just go finish inventory." She laughs as she walks away, giving me the bird.

I pull my phone out from my pocket, unlocking it to type in my mom's name.

ME:

> Hey, I completely forgot to bring you your food Tuesday evening. I'm so sorry! I'll swing by after work.

I put my phone back and grab my pencil, and begin to mark down the coffee creamers.

I've been running around the house for the past few days, getting it cleaned and prepared for my trip. Eric thinks I need to chill out, telling me the house is fine and will continue to be fine when we are gone. But if I don't do anything now, I'll do it all the day before, which also means I will sit all day and do nothing because I have all these uncompleted tasks that I still have yet to do.

I was diagnosed with ADHD years ago, though I didn't know what it meant at the time. My parents noticed I was a bit different from the other kids and took me to a specialist.

I don't recall what tests were done then, but I remember it was the first grade, and I was having a hard time that school year. Staying still was challenging and focusing on composure made it harder. Teachers believed they were helping by assigning me to the back of the class, but being back there just allowed me to get more distracted. My demeanor grew increasingly shy and awkward, and any attempts to form friendships resulted in eventual abandonment. Once I recognized their abandonment, I struggled to articulate my feelings.

Then, in the third grade, I met Scarlett. Her hair was in pigtails, and her small voice asked me, out of all people, for a pencil because she didn't like the other kids and their attitudes toward me. I thought it was a joke, maybe a dare from someone to speak to me, but nothing bad happened after that conversation.

We began hanging out at lunch and recess and even on the weekends, which turned into sleepovers at each other's house every week. From that moment on, we were like two peas in a pod.

"Hey, want to come over on Saturday?" Scarlett asks, interrupting my thoughts.

I look at the time, not realizing it's already five o'clock.

"Sure! What are we doing?"

"Movie night, I was thinking a romantic movie of some sort," she says as she locks the café's front door.

"Sounds fun, I'll see ya!" I say, giving her a hug.

"Bye!" She waves, and we both get into our cars.

I grab my key and unlock the front door of my mom's house; the soft glow of the evening sun filters through the stained glass window, casting colorful patterns on the floor. She's going to be so happy about the soup I'm bringing. Hopefully, it makes up for missing it last time.

"Mom!" I holler while closing the door behind me. A gust of wind sweeps in, carrying with it the scent of freshly cut grass.

I step into the cozy living room, the familiar scent of lavender and vanilla wafting through the air. As I make my way toward the kitchen, my eyes catch a glimpse of the family photos adorning the walls—a visual timeline of cherished memories.

I find Mom curled up on the couch, wrapped in a warm blanket. She looks up from her book, her eyes brightening as a smile graces her face.

"There you are, sweetheart!" she exclaims, setting the book aside. "I was just getting in to this novel and lost track of time."

I smile back, setting the bag with the soup container on the coffee table. "Well, I brought something to warm you up. Chicken noodle soup, just the way you like it."

Her eyes light up even more, and she pats the spot next to her on the couch. "You're always taking care of me. What would I do without you?"

I take a seat beside her, the warmth of the blanket enveloping us both. "You'd manage just fine, Mom. But I can't resist spoiling you a bit."

She chuckles softly, reaching for the bag. "Spoil away, my dear. I could use some pampering today."

I hand her the soup container, and the rich aroma fills the room. Steam rises when she lifts the lid, carrying the comforting scent of homemade goodness. Mom takes a tentative spoonful and sighs with satisfaction.

"Oh, this is heavenly. You really know how to make a sick woman feel better."

I lean back, content to watch her enjoy the soup. "I'm just glad I could make it up to you. I know I spaced and forgot to bring some the other day."

Mom sets the container aside and places a hand on mine. "Life gets busy, sweetheart. I understand. But you being here now is all that matters. Besides, I've missed our talks."

Between spoonfuls of soup, Mom looks at me with a curious glint in her eyes. "You've been smiling like the cat that got the cream all evening. What's going on, Hailey?"

I try to suppress my grin but fail miserably.

"Eric's taking me to Hawaii."

Her jaw drops, and she nearly spills her soup. "Hawaii? Are you serious?"

I nod, barely able to contain my excitement. "Yes, Mom. He's been secretly planning it and surprised me with it last week."

She claps her hands like a giddy schoolgirl.

"Oh, Hailey, that's incredible! You've always wanted to go there," she says before sneezing into her arm.

"Oh, Mom, I love you, but maybe I should go before I get sick and am unable to go on the trip."

"Wait, when is it?"

"We leave Monday."

"Monday? That's just a few days away!" Mom exclaims, a mix of surprise and joy coloring her words.

"Make sure to pack emergency items," Mom advises between sniffles. "And don't forget your camera. You'll want to capture every moment!"

I nod, grateful for her support and guidance. Despite the imminent departure, there's a twinge of concern for her. "Are you sure you'll be okay while I'm gone, Mom?"

She smiles weakly. "Of course, sweetheart. I'll be fine. This is your chance to explore and experience new things. Don't worry about me. Besides, I have the whole house to myself. Maybe I'll finally finish that book I started last year!"

"I wish Ray was here to keep you company," I whisper.

"He's here in my heart, baby girl."

CHAPTER EIGHT

Friday is here, and the games will begin in a couple of hours. Eric is still at work but as soon as he gets off, he's heading home to shower to prepare for game night.

"Scarlett, get your ass over here." This woman has been bouncing off the walls today. She's giddy and excited for her date tonight, but damn, she's just all over the place.

"What?" she asks as she walks over to me.

"Customers are looking at you like you're on something," I say, crossing my arms.

"What? No, they aren't," she says as she looks around, only to see some people staring.

"Can't a girl be excited about a date?" she says out loud while looking at me. Making sure people hear her.

"Well, yes, you can but, girl, you have bumped into a table a few times already and dropped two plates of food before it got to a customer." I laugh

She frowns. "I'm just nervous. I'm sorry."

"You're going to be fine."

"I'll tone it down a bit. Love you!"

I shake my head with a grin. "Love you!"

She's such a good person, and I know Zack is nice, but her heart is fragile. If she's this excited about a guy, I worry about how she'll react if her heart is broken into pieces. My phone buzzes. I pull it from my pocket and unlock it.

Eric

Hey baby, I will be getting off work early because of the storm rolling in.

The curve of my lips goes up, and I let out a quiet squeal. I love it when he's off work early.

Me

Okay, see you soon, drive safe.

I glance out the window and see the sun hides above the clouds, and it's beginning to darken. Game night is much more fun when thunder roars in the sky.

"Hey, did you share the prize online yet?"

Scarlett asks me, tray of dirty dishes in hand.

"Oh shit. No, I'll do it now."

"Don't make me regret having you host!" She chuckles and walks to the back, heading toward the kitchen. She's something else.

The day she told me about wanting to own a café, I thought she was nuts. She came over banging on the door, and as soon as I opened it, she just spilled all this stuff about opening a café and making a community out of it. We spent all night coming up with ways to make it inviting. We were watching the Super Bowl when we came up with "game night." Our game nights aren't related to football, but it's still fun for everyone.

"Have fun on your date!" I holler as Scarlett leaves.

She waves at me, and I walk back inside. She helped me clean up, so I make sure all the games are set up on each table. Thunder roars, making me jump. I love storms, but damn, thunder can be very loud and come out of nowhere. The door chimes, and I look up to see Eric and grin. I walk quickly to him, erasing the space between us, and throw my arms around his neck, giving him a kiss.

"Hi, baby!" I exclaim.

"Hi!" he says while wrapping his arms around my waist.

"I missed you." I look into blue eyes. *Oh, they are so beautiful.*

"I missed you, too."

"People should be showing up soon."

"Let's hope, I really don't need people coming in soaked."

He looks at his phone. "The weather app says it's not supposed to rain for another half hour."

I look out and see a few cars pulling in, their bright headlights nearly blinding me.

"Well, look at that. People have arrived," I say.

I open the door and set a rock in front of it for it to stay open.

"Come on in, everyone! Game night is about to start!" I say.

More cars pull in. This will be fun.

After about twenty minutes, everyone is finally here and in their seats, getting ready for a game.

"Help me up on the counter, please?" I ask Eric as I pass by him.

"What? Why?"

"I need to make the game and prize announcement."

"On the counter?" he asks.

"Yes, on the counter, dummy!" I smile, crossing my arms.

With a smile, he shakes his head, his laughter filling the room, and says, "Okay." He effortlessly lifts me off the floor and gently places me on the counter.

With a playful wink, I say, "Do that again."

"Love you," he says.

I stand on the counter. "Alrighty, everyone, listen up!" I command attention. "The first table to finish all five board games wins a trip to Disney World!"

The crowd of people cheer.

"Remember to tap the bell on the table when you finish the games!"

As soon as I finish my sentence, the room buzzes with the excitement of the upcoming game night. Everyone eagerly grabs their respective games, laughter and chatter filling the air. "Disney World?" Eric's voice cuts through the lively atmosphere, catching my attention. I look up to see him standing there, a hopeful smile playing on his lips.

"Yeah," I reply with a grin. "Scarlett got two tickets for tonight. It's going to be amazing."

His eyes light up with genuine enthusiasm. "I haven't been to Disney since I was a kid."

I feel a warmth in my chest at the thought

of sharing this experience with him. "Aw, we'll definitely have to plan a trip together soon," I say, finding a free table and taking a seat. Eric joins me, sitting across from me, and the soft melody fills the background, creating a cozy atmosphere.

"I called my mom earlier," he suddenly reveals, his tone shifting slightly.

My excitement wavers, and I sense an unexpected tension creeping into the conversation. I look at him, waiting for more details. The air between us thickens, and my curiosity heightens.

"How's she doing?" I ask cautiously, not sure why his mom would be a source of tension.

Eric's expression tightens, and for a moment, he seems lost in thought. "She's been going through a tough time lately," he confesses, his gaze dropping to the table as if unwilling to meet my eyes.

My heart sinks as I realize the shift in the evening's mood. I search for the right words to offer support, unsure of the depth of Eric's feelings about his mom.

"I'm sorry to hear that," I say gently, reaching across the table to touch his hand. "Is there anything I can do to help support you both?"

The room around us fades as the gravity of Eric's words settles in, casting a shadow over the promising night.

Eric looks up, his eyes reflecting a mixture of gratitude and vulnerability. The connection between us deepens as the weight of his concerns becomes palpable in the air.

"It's just that," he says, his voice tinged with hesitation, "tomorrow is the anniversary of my dad's passing, and I'm not there to help her."

Eric's words hang heavy in the air, and the room seems to dim as the reality of the situation sinks in.

"I'm so sorry," I murmur, the gravity of the moment weighing on me. His gaze meets mine, and I see a mixture of sadness and frustration in his eyes.

"When we get to my house, let's call her."

"Okay," he says softly.

The rain begins to pitter-patter on the roof, and it gets louder as it pours heavy. "Looks like no one will be going home until this dies down," I say.

The game bell rings, and I look over at a table a few rows away.

"Oh my gosh! Our table won!" a man in a red shirt says, standing with his arms in the air in victory.

I grab the tickets from my purse and hand them to Eric. "Give the man his prize." I smile.

He nods and walks over to him, handing him the tickets, and they shake hands.

CHAPTER NINE

I WAKE UP TO THE SOFT MORNING LIGHT STREAMING through the curtains, casting a warm glow in the bedroom. Something feels off about today. Eric is still sound asleep beside me. I can't help but smile as I watch him, peaceful and content. Unless he works, Saturdays are our lazy days, and today is no exception. I gently nudge him awake.

"Hi," he says as his eyes flutter open.

"Hi," I say, giving him a kiss. "I'm going into the kitchen for coffee. Do you want some?" I ask.

"Yes, please."

I throw the covers off my legs and stand, grabbing my hair tie from the nightstand and pulling my hair into a high ponytail.

I slip into my robe and make my way into the kitchen. My routine begins with the familiar motions of preparing the coffeepot—grabbing a filter, adding water, and spooning in the coffee grounds. As the aromatic brew starts, I settle into a chair at the table, anticipating the comforting warmth of the first sip.

"Shit, I forgot my wallet at the café," I mutter to myself.

"Morning, beautiful," Eric greets, entering the room shirtless.

"Well, hey there," I reply, a smile playing on my lips. I grab two mugs, place them next to the coffeepot, and pour coffee into each one.

I place two tablespoons of sugar in mine, mixing it up, and leaving Eric's black, just the way he likes it.

"Here." I hand him his and sit.

As we sip our coffee, I couldn't shake the nagging thought about Eric's mom. "Hey, when are you planning to call your mom?" I ask, trying not to sound too concerned.

Eric glances at the clock and replies, "I'll probably give her a call this afternoon."

I nod.

After a little while, Eric gets up and places his mug in the sink, rinsing it out.

"Want to do something today?" he suggests.

An idea pops into my mind. "How about we go for a ride in the Jeep?" I propose, hoping to infuse a sense of adventure into our day.

Eric looks at me, eyes wide. "The Jeep? You

haven't touched it since Ray passed away."

I take a deep breath. "I know, but I think I'm ready to enjoy it again. Let's make new memories with it. What do you say?"

A soft smile forms on his lips. "All right, let's do it."

The crisp breeze from the Carolina shore sweeps through the open Jeep, carrying with it the unmistakable scent of salt water. I grip the wheel, feeling the familiar hum of the engine resonating beneath my fingertips. Beside me, Eric adjusts his seat, settling in for the ride.

The coastal road stretches ahead, winding through picturesque landscapes and offering glimpses of the shimmering ocean. As we drive, the scent of the sea mingles with the fragrance of blooming wildflowers, creating a sensory symphony that dances through the air. I can't help but steal glances at Eric, the sunlight playing on his features, highlighting the warmth in his eyes.

The music, a blend of our favorite tunes, fills the Jeep, drowning out the world outside. The wind tousles my hair, and I close my eyes, immersing myself in the moment.

I turn to Eric, a smile playing on his lips, and shout over the wind, "Isn't this fun?"

He grins back, his eyes reflecting the same sense of wonder. "It's like a breath of fresh air," I reply, the wind carrying my words away.

As the Jeep cruises along the coastal road, a gentle reminder of my forgotten wallet creeps into my thoughts.

"Hey, I need to stop by the café and grab my wallet. Totally forgot earlier," I say.

Eric flashes a reassuring smile. "No problem. Let's swing by."

I turn the corner, and soon, we arrive at the café. "I'll be right back."

I walk to the door, unlocking it, and step inside only to see Scarlett and Zack making out on the counter. They both jump and look at me with wide eyes. I raise my hands up slightly. "Ya know what, I wasn't here." I chuckle.

"Why are you here on your day off?"

I raise my brows. "I forgot my wallet from game night."

"Hi, Hailey," Zack says with a wave.

"Hi." I press my lips together, giving a small wave back, and head toward the employee room. As I retrieve my wallet next to the computer, I notice the envelope my dad mailed me. I thought I threw it out. What the fuck? I snatch it and stuff it in my pocket, then hurry out the door.

"Bye, love ya, Scar, see you next week. Bye, Zack!"

"Bye, Hails, love ya, have fun!" Scarlett hollers back as I rush toward the Jeep.

"Why is your face so flushed?" Eric asks me as I climb into the seat.

"I witnessed Zack and Scarlett in a heated make-out session."

"Oh, that's awkward," he says.

"Yeah..." I pull out of the parking lot.

"Wanna make out when we get back?"

Thank God for the breeze going through my hair the way it is because I can feel the heat in my face right now.

"Sure." I laugh and turn the radio up.

"I'm going to take a bath," I mention, hanging the keys on the rack.

"At noon? Are you sure?" he asks.

"I just need to clear my head," I reply, lowering my gaze.

"What's going on, sweetheart?" He approaches me and gently lifts my chin.

I let out a shaky breath and pull out the envelope from my pocket. "My dad mailed this to my work. I haven't even opened it yet."

"Mind if I see it?" he asks.

"Sure, just, uh, don't open it, I really don't want to focus on whatever it says."

He nods, and I hand it to him. He places it in his back pocket and wraps his arms around me, kissing the top of my head.

"I love you so much. Get some rest. I'll be in the living room if you need me, okay?"

I nod, looking up at him as he gives me a kiss, grabs a drink, and heads to the living room.

I bite my quivering lip, take a deep breath, and prepare for my bath. I haven't had a stress bath since before I cut my dad off, and I really need it right now.

CHAPTER TEN

THE FLIGHT TO HAWAII WAS LONG, BUT SO WORTH THE wait.

"Babe, the plane's landed," Eric whispers, pushing a strand of hair out of my face, behind my ear. Oh boy. I hold my stomach and clutch my purse. Eric stands, gesturing for me to take his hand. I grasp it tightly and stand slowly.

"You all right?" he asks.

"Yeah, just glad we are on land now." I yawn.

"I told you that you'd be okay." He lets go of my hand and grabs his phone charger and plops it into his duffel bag, then takes my hand again, intertwining his with mine.

"Yeah, in the midst of my panic attack."

"Hey, I love you. I'm here, and it's all right."

I close my eyes and take a deep breath. "Let's go."

Time flies by with a nap, that's for sure. I've never been on a plane before, it's such a cool yet scary experience. Heights are not my thing.

The sun hangs low in the sky, bringing a warm glow over Daniel K. Inouye International Airport. Eric flashes me a smile as we walk hand in hand toward the entrance. My stomach eases, and I lean my head on his arm. After about an hour and a half, we finally got to the Turtle Bay Resort.

"This place is so pretty," I say as I look up at the hotel.

"Not as pretty as you," he says with a cheeky smile. "Come on, let's check in." He places his arm around my waist, and we go through the main entrance. The inside is absolutely breathtaking, like nothing I've ever seen before. My face is beginning to ache with all the smiling I'm doing; I can't help it, though. We get checked in, grab our keys, and head up to our floor.

"Ready?" he asks.

"Yes," I say with childlike excitement.

He unlocks the door with the key card, turning the door handle to let me through. I walk in, and the first thing I see is the view of the crystal blue ocean."Oh my gosh!" I squeal as I reach the glass windows.

"You like it?" he asks as he rolls our suitcases by the bed.

"Yes, it's perfect. We have our own little backyard and patio too!"

"I figured you'd want this type of view," he whispers in my ear, wrapping his arms around my waist from behind.

"I love you," I say, slightly tilting my head and closing my eyes as he kisses my neck.

"How about you and I go out for dinner tonight?"

The feeling of goosebumps takes over my body when he whispers in my ear with his deep voice.

"Sure, where to?" I ask.

I squeal as he spins me around to face him. I look into his eyes, and he smiles.

"It's a surprise."

"Oh, okay." I flirt.

"Let's go get in a swimsuit, and we will head right out to the beach, okay?" he asks.

"Can we grab something to eat first?" My stomach rumbles loudly, causing me to pout and place my hand over it.

"I'm hungry too," he says softly, leaning in closer. "For you…" he whispers, his lips brushing against mine as he kisses me.

Gently biting my lip, he pulls away. "I want more of those kisses."

"Nope, get ready so we can go out."

"Fine," I whine.

I savor every bite of my delicious chicken sandwich, a grin spreading across my face. "This is so good!" It is the perfect way to end our first day in Hawaii.

"Gotta try making this at home," he says,

I nod while taking a refreshing sip of my ice-cold Pepsi. My gaze wanders to the breathtaking ocean view from our spot at the bar and grill. This vacation is a much-needed escape.

Shifting my focus to Eric, I can't help but be captivated by his radiant smile, accentuated by those irresistible dimples and the twinkle in his eyes, reflecting the sun's warmth. Moments like these make me appreciate having him in my life, like a scene from a Nicholas Sparks novel coming to life.

Our conversation is momentarily interrupted by a familiar ding from my phone—a text from Scarlett.

SCARLETT

Hey, how's it going? Miss you!

We both read the message together and can't help but laugh, finding Scarlett's sentiment absolutely endearing.

"Let's capture this moment for her and us," he suggests. I rise from my seat, and he taps his lap. A slight blush warms my cheeks as I settle onto his lap. Switching my phone to selfie mode, I fumble with the angle to ensure we capture the perfect shot.

Eric wraps his arms around me in a slow, comforting motion, planting a soft, warm kiss on my cheek. With a smile on my face, I quickly snap the photo, cherishing the sweetness and cuteness encapsulated in that moment.

"The sunset brings out your radiant glow," he murmurs softly, and I can't help but smile.

"Ready to head back to the hotel?" I ask.

"Yeah, baby," he says,

I get up from his lap and settle back into my chair.

"Ma'am, can I get the check, please?" he politely asks the passing server.

"Sure can, give me a moment," she replies before walking away.

As I unlock my phone, feeling the smooth touch of the screen beneath my fingertips, I quickly attach the photo before typing a response to Scarlett,

ME

It's going amazing! Miss you too!

"Here's the check," the server hands it to him.

He hands them his card, and we wait for her to come back with it.

Once she does, she hands him a receipt, and we make our way back toward the hotel. Not caring about our unpacked luggage, we both undress and climb into bed. As soon as my head hits the pillow, I'm off to dreamland.

CHAPTER ELEVEN

THE SECOND DAY OF OUR VACATION IS HERE, AND I'M MORE excited than ever. I let out a heavy sigh while fumbling with the back of my bikini top. "Stupid fucking strings," I mutter to myself.

"Here, baby, let me help."

I let go of the strings. "Thank you."

"Maybe we should get you a bikini with a bra connection for the back," he suggests.

Hm. Maybe.

"I didn't even know that was a thing for swimsuits."

"Well, when we get back home, we'll order you a couple to try."

I shrug. *I don't know. I don't think I even look the greatest in swimsuits.*

"Yeah, that'll be fine."

I throw my hair up into a bun. "Let's go sunbathe for a bit." I grab a towel and walk out into the backyard the hotel room offers.

This place is freaking gorgeous! I quickly snap a photo of the ocean view behind the backyard, adjust the contrast a little, and share it on my social media before setting my phone back down.

"How about we go on a boat tonight?"

"Sounds fun!"

"Well, let's relax for now, and I'll set it up soon," he says, playing on his phone.

With a smile, I open my e-reader and continue the book I was reading.

"Close your eyes," he says. I follow his lead, and we walk for a bit. Suddenly, a "woosh" sound breaks the quietness surrounding me.

"Open."

I open my eyes and am immediately captivated by a helicopter landing right in front of us.

"Whoa! Really?" I ask.

"Yes, really. I want us to have the best experience we can while here," he says.

Ah, the pieces are coming together. Keeping the belongings back at the hotel was intentional for this surprise helicopter ride. It's all making sense now. "This is why you told me to keep my purse and stuff back at the hotel."

He nods. "Ready?"

"I'm a nervous wreck, but I have this."

He hands me a headset, and I place it over my ears before sitting in a seat.

My heart feels like it's about to implode, and I squeeze his hand as the helicopter takes off.

Next time I come here, I want to bring my mom and Scarlett. They would have a blast. When I peer downward at the ocean, I'm struck by the seamless movement of its blue-green color as it gently rolls through the waves. I grip my belt once the helicopter glides sideways a bit, and I feel a hand on mine. "You okay?" Eric mouths to me once I turn to face him.

I nod. "I'm hanging in there."

"Hey look, dolphins!" He points out.

I look out and see five dolphins swimming through the ocean waves. "Oh my God! That's so cool!"

It's neat seeing all the green land from above. There's so much land, so much adventure to be sought.

"Can we take a photo?" I ask the pilot.

"Yes, go right ahead!"

I take my phone out of my pocket and open the camera app. "Say cheese, Eric!"

"Cheese," we both say and smile. I snap a photo and send it to Scarlett before placing my phone back in my pocket.

"That was so fun! I want to do it again sometime." I exclaim, grabbing Eric's hand as we head back into the hotel room.

"Yeah? I'm glad. I had fun too."

"Are we going on a boat today?" I ask in a flirty tone, wrapping my arms around his neck and looking into his eyes.

"I don't know, are we?" He grins.

"What should I wear?"

"Anything you're comfortable in."

I playfully roll my eyes. "I was hoping you'd pick something out for me." I stick my bottom lip out.

"Fine, how about you wear that white blouse and your jean shorts?"

"Okay, deal."

"Better get ready within the hour. I'll be back soon," he says while walking to the front door of the hotel room.

"Where are you going?" I ask.

"Setting up our boat date." He winks, and walks out the door.

As I retrieve my shirt and shorts from the suitcase, thoughts of Scarlett's recent words flood my mind. Is he planning to propose? Could she already be aware? The idea of marrying this man fills me with joy. I enter the bathroom, shedding my shirt and leggings, and step into the shower, where the hot water quickly envelops me. I take a moment to savor the warmth of the water.

I reach for my shampoo. I made sure to bring my own as the hotel ones usually suck. A hollow feeling flows through my chest as I think about home. I've never been away from home before, not this far. I sigh and blink away the tears that've been trying to escape. I used to get homesick as a kid a lot when I visited my dad. I didn't see his house as my home like Mom and Ray's.

I rinse the shampoo, apply conditioner, and begin scrubbing my body with my lavender-scented soap before rinsing, grabbing the towel, and wrapping it around my body.

Looking in the mirror, I see a girl who's been lost for ages, tired of the chaos, but also a mix of happiness because she's found love, found someone who cares about her and is patient with her. I take the blow-dryer that's already installed here and dry my hair. I think I may just do a french braid from the top. I dress into my blouse and shorts, add a touch of lip gloss, mascara, and pomade brow gel. Putting the makeup back down, I head into the living room only to see a bouquet of red roses and an envelope on the bed.

I pick up the note and open it.

I know you're taking your sweet time in the shower, so I figured I'd set this down before you come out fully ready. I need you to come down to the beach, where we had the picnic earlier. I'll be waiting. I love you. – Eric.

A soft smile plays on my lips, and I can't help but nibble on them, feeling a warmth creeping into my cheeks. Gently, I set the note down, and my fingers lovingly trace its edges. Then, with a tender touch, I lift the roses, their fragrance enveloping me like a sweet embrace. Tilting my head back, I close my eyes and inhale deeply.

As I reach the beach, I spot a flickering glow in the distance. I walk closer, discovering a picturesque scene. Eric has set up a dreamy picnic amid the golden hues of the sunset. Faux candles twinkle on a blanket, a basket of delectable treats awaits, and there he stands, a silhouette against the breathtaking backdrop.

"Being with you," he says, his voice soft, "has been the greatest adventure of my life. Every moment with you is like catching a glimpse of eternity. I've never been more sure about anything."

He reaches into his pocket, and my heart

skips a beat. The anticipation hangs in the air, and as he pulls out a small dark blue box, I feel my breath catch.

"When I walked into that café, I didn't realize I was about to meet the love of my life. When I first met you, I was drawn in immediately by your crystal blue eyes."

My lip quivers. I can't speak.

He takes my hand, my knees feel weak, and my stomach flutters with butterflies like crazy.

"I want to be with you for the rest of my life. I want to wake up to your messy, beautiful hair that you dislike so much. I want to wrap my arms around you every single moment I can while I'm with you."

Opening it, he reveals a stunning ring that glimmers in the fading sunlight. He gets down on one knee. This is actually happening.

"Will you marry me?"

I nod. "Yes, I will." A big grin appears on his face as he glides the ring on my finger. I hug him tightly and let the tears fall from my eyes with a mix of laughter.

"I love you so much!" he whispers into my ear as he holds me close.

"I love you too."

"Let's eat, and we can go on that boat."

"I don't know if I can eat. My emotions are crazy right now."

"You can't say no to these chocolate strawberries. They will be offended," he says sarcastically.

"Okay, you've convinced me."

CHAPTER TWELVE

The breeze blows through my hair as I sit on the back patio, gazing at the ocean. I keep glancing at my ring and the water. I don't want to seem like I'm obsessing over a ring, but I can't help but admire how beautiful the princess cut is. Scar will freak, but I don't want to show her first through a photo. I'll wait until we are home to show her in person.

"Hey, babe, look at Scarlett and Zack's post," Eric says.

I take a look at his phone screen and laugh. The two of them are making a mess in the café kitchen. Flour is all over the place.

"I'm so glad she's happy," I say as I look over the photo.

"Has she never been in a relationship before?"

"Yeah, but nothing serious. Most men just wanted to know her rich dad more than anything," I say.

"What? Why?" he asks.

I shrug. "Because he owns five boathouses, which a lot of college kids try to get in free by dating her."

"That's fucked up."

"Yup."

"Well, Zack isn't the type. I grew up with him."

"You guys are best friends, or...?"

"No, just close friends. We kind of grew apart when I moved as a kid, but we still kept in contact."

"That's good. I mean, he seems like a nice guy, but I've had many nights when she'd call me crying her eyes out over a guy telling her how they were using her, and it's just a whole ordeal I'd rather her not have to deal with again."

"I'm sorry, Hails," he says, giving me a hug.

My phone rings, and I look to see it's my mom.

"Hello?" I answer.

"Hey, honey, do you got a sec?" my mom asks, and I can hear her voice shaking.

"Yeah, what's wrong?"

"I didn't want to tell you while you were still on vacation, but I would rather tell you first than you finding out another way," she says. My heart drops.

"What is it?" I ask. Eric looks at me, his head cocked to the side with an expression of concern.

"Your dad, he's dead."

My heart has definitely sunk to the pits of my stomach. Tears begin to form, but I blink them away. With a shaky breath, I say, "I'll call you back."

I end the call, place my phone on the glass table, and walk back into the hotel room. Eric calls out for me, but I'm so numb I'm not processing his words.

I hurry into the bathroom, closing and locking the door behind me, and undress for a stress bath. Eric knocks repeatedly at the door. "Let me be for an hour, please!" I holler. And he stops.

Sitting in the tub as it fills with water, I stare blankly at the wall in front of me, biting my lip and trying not to burst into tears. But forcing them down makes it worse, and I shake uncontrollably, crying out. My face is warm, and I can already tell it's red and blotchy without having to look in a mirror. He's dead? How can this be? I don't understand.

First, my stepdad, and now my biological dad? Granted, he treated me like shit, but that doesn't mean I want him dead. I officially have no father. I'm fatherless. I'm nothing. Why is he gone? Why are they both gone? What did I fucking do to deserve this? Shit, the letter I received.

Was it something from my dad about his death? Oh my God, I'm such a piece of shit daughter for not reading it.

The bathroom door opens, and I see Eric come in from the corner of my eye, but I don't look at him. I locked the door so I'm not sure how he got in. But I'm glad he did. I bring my knees up to my chest. The water has already halfway filled the tub. Eric turns the water off and ties my hair into a bun. He always knows what I need.

I look up at him and begin crying again as I stare into his eyes. I notice his lip quivers, and he gets in the tub with me while fully clothed. He holds me close, and I cry hard into his chest.

"I'm so sorry," I say through my cries.

"Sorry for what, baby?" he asks.

"For this happening while on our vacation."

"Shhh, I love you. Don't be sorry." He holds me tighter, and I continue crying until it tires me out.

"I'd like to go to bed early, if that's okay?" I ask.

"Sure, baby, come on," he says, getting out of the tub and lifting me from it. He didn't even bother undressing when he got in the tub, so his clothes are soaked. He grabs a towel, wraps it around me, and walks me into the bedroom. Using one hand to place a towel over the bed, he lays me on it. He grabs another towel and dries me off, then places the sheet over me, and I drift off to sleep.

My eyes slightly burn when I open them, my head feels foggy, and I notice it's dark out. Getting up slowly, I turn to find Eric and see him reading with the small lamp on his bedside table.

"Hi," I whisper with a groggy voice.

He looks at me with a small smile and places his book down.

"Hi, baby, how are you feeling?"

"Like I got hit by a truck."

"I ordered room service about an hour ago. I figured you'd want something simple to eat tonight, so I got you that grilled chicken sandwich you like and some Pepsi," he says.

I look over at the tray of food, and my stomach growls. "I could eat right now."

He chuckles. "Sounds like it."

I sit up, and he hands me my plate and drink.

"Your mom called me soon after you went into the bathroom."

Oh great.

"What'd she say?" I ask, taking a sip of my drink. Of course she's going to call him to make sure I'm okay.

"What she told you, and she was worried about you."

"Can we just not talk about any of this right now? I just want to enjoy my time here before we have to leave tomorrow," I snap.

He looks at me as if I just broke his favorite thing in the world.

"I'm sorry," I whisper.

"It's okay, I understand." He lies on his side, running his fingertips over my back while I eat.

My breath is shaky. I feel like I just finished running a marathon, and the energy in my body is gone. I finish my meal and head to the bathroom, closing the door behind me. Stepping toward the sink, I look in the mirror. My face is tearstained and still slightly blotchy and red. I flip the faucet on and lean over to splash cold water on my face a couple of times. I understand why my mom told me while on vacation. I just wish the situation never happened at all.

I quickly dry my face and head back into the room. Eric lifts the covers, and I give a small smile and snuggle into his chest. He drapes the blanket back over me, and I fall asleep again.

The airport lobby is pretty much dead this morning. Good, because I really don't feel like dealing with more chaos than I already have. I sit on the chair while waiting for Eric to be done in the bathroom. I grab my phone from my pocket and tap Scarlett's name.

ME

Are you on the way?

SCARLETT

Yeah, I'm five minutes out.

I don't get why she's late. She could've been here before we were.

Eric walks out of the bathroom and sits beside me. "No Scarlett?" he asks.

"She's five minutes out, apparently." I sigh. I just want the day to be over already. He lays his arm over my shoulders, and I lean into his chest while we wait.

I'm scared of what the next few days and weeks will be like. I don't handle bad news well, and this kind of news is taking a toll on me physically and mentally. Every little thing is bothering me. I probably should make an appointment with a therapist before I feel worse.

"Hi, guys!" Scarlett greets us cheerfully

and wraps me in a hug.

"Hi," I say. She gives Eric a hug as well.

"Let me see that ring." She takes my hand, and her eyes widen. "Damn, dude, you did well!" I know she knows what's going on. This is her way of making the light shine into the darkness.

"Well, let's get going so we can rest," Eric says and grabs the handle of his suitcase. Scarlett takes mine. Eric holds my hand, and we leave out the exit doors and settle into Scarlett's car.

I can't get over the thought of what could've happened or the what-ifs with my dad. I feel so guilty and mad at myself for cutting him out of my life. I know what he's done to me, and I know I had to do what was best for me, but I still feel like shit. You never know when your last day on earth will be.

While tying my hair into a pony, I notice the envelope next to me on the nightstand. With a shaky hand, I grab it and look over my dad's handwriting, and shed a tear before opening it.

Hailey, by the time you get this letter, I'll be gone from this world.

I blink away the tears coming through.

We've not spoken for nearly a year, and I'm to blame for that. I wish things were different. I wish I could take back everything I've ever said and put you through.

I cover my mouth, trying to quiet my sobs.

I love you. May we meet again.

As I read those words, a lump forms in my throat, and the weight of regret settles heavily on my chest. The room seems to close in around me, and the air feels thick with sorrow. I trace my fingers over the ink on the paper, as if seeking a connection with the dad I've kept at arm's length.

The room is silent, except for the muffled sounds of my own sobs. Each sentence in the letter feels like a dagger piercing through the walls I've built to protect myself. A flood of memories rushes back, both the painful moments and the ones tinged with love and warmth.

"I'm sorry," I whisper, as if he can hear me from beyond. But the apology isn't just for him; it's for me, for the guilt I bear for shutting him out. I fold the letter carefully and place it back on my nightstand.

The reality of his absence sinks in, and the room feels colder, lonelier. I bury my face in my hands, fingers entangled in my hair, and let the tears flow freely.

I get up and stumble toward the bathroom, my vision blurry by my tears. The tile floor feels cold beneath my feet as I reach the edge of the bathtub. Without a second thought, I undress, step into the empty tub, and turn the water on. Bringing my knees to my chest, I wrap my arms around my legs.

I sit here, knees drawn up to my chest, shoulders shaking with each heartbreaking sob. My tub is where I can release emotions that have been pent up for far too long.

CHAPTER THIRTEEN

I look down at my ring, and my chin begins to tremble. One second, I'm happily eating the food Eric made, and the next, I'm pissed off for God knows what. It's been weeks since I found out about my dad dying, and I also found out my fucking family on that side had a funeral without me knowing, without inviting his own blood daughter to it. I kept trying to contact them, but I've had no luck. My moods have been awful since the news of his death.

"Can you please stop? I love you so much!"

"You love me and will eventually leave like he has."

"Don't compare me to him! I'm not the one who's been hurting you. I've been nothing but supportive. Why are you trying to push me away?" Eric shouts.

"Supportive? You call this support?" I yell, throwing my living room remote across the hall. "Maybe I'm just so used to being verbally attacked, and I can't see the difference anymore," I whisper more to myself than anyone else.

"Stop throwing shit! I'm not your dad, and I won't let you treat me like him. I've been patient, understanding, and all I get is your anger out of fucking nowhere!"

Oh fucking whatever.

"Your patience is a facade. You'll get tired of me, just like he has. It's only a matter of time."

"If I get tired of you, then I clearly didn't get enough sleep! I'll take a damn nap, and I'll be fine!"

"You are a pain in my ass!" My ears pound alongside my heart, and my throat becomes more dry each time I yell.

"If I wasn't, I don't know how this relationship could work!"

I look at him, brows raised. "Oh, so you're saying there's a chance it might not?"

"Oh, I'm always going to be a pain in your ass, just like you're one in mine."

In the heat of the argument, as the tension reaches its peak, the room falls silent. We stare at each other. We've never fought before.

I take a deep breath. "You know what? Maybe I need some sleep. I'm exhausted."

"Yeah, you look tired. Just get some sleep," he says.

I scoff and walk into my room, slamming

the door behind me and lie down in bed.

"Hails, honey, wake up," a soft voice says near me. I open my eyes to see Scarlett sitting beside me, placing my hair behind my ear.

"Where's Eric?" I ask, sitting up.

"He's at work. He told me what's going on at home, and I took off work for the week to spend time with you."

I shake my head. "No offense, Scar, but our relationship has nothing to do with you."

"I never said it did, but you're my best friend. I'm here for you, always, no matter what."

"Why can't he be here if he felt that way?"

"He said he's already missed too much work. He'll be here when he gets off work," she says calmly.

"What about the shop? You can't just close it."

"I own the place. I can do whatever." She laughs.

"Yeah, yeah, I know. But I need to get out of the house and work sounds like a nice excuse right now."

"You're not in the right headspace to be

working. Just rest this week, please?"

Ah, good ole Scarlett just being caring and controlling at the same time.

"Whatever," I say and stand, heading to the kitchen. I go to open the fridge door when I see a business card attached to it. "Dr. Ashlyn Kale, THERAPIST at Ole Town," I whisper aloud.

I snatch it from my fridge and turn around. "What is this?" I demand.

"I booked you an appointment to talk to someone."

"I can't afford to see a doctor. Why the hell would I go?"

"For one, I'm going to pay for it. And two, you need it."

"No, I just want to be left the fuck alone. Why can't you just leave. Me. Alone!" I yell, throwing the card at her.

I don't care if I'm acting like a child. I just don't want to deal with anyone or anything right now.

"Hailey, please stop. You know deep inside it's something you need. I won't force you to go, but at least think about it."

I look at her right as I grab the doorknob. "The way you push about it makes me wonder if you're the one who fucking needs it." I glare, swinging the front door open and slamming it behind me as I walk out.

The beach has always been my second calming space, similar to my bathtub, except I'm not naked. I sit on the sandy shore, gazing out at the water. The beauty of this moment is timeless, especially as noon approaches and the sun's rays illuminate the waves, transforming them into a sparkling spectacle reminiscent of diamonds.

I unlock my phone and tap on Eric's name.

ME

I'm sorry. I love you.

He won't see it for a couple of hours since he cannot have his phone until breaks and lunch.

Ray would tell me it's okay to be upset, but to take it out on others isn't fair. "I'm sorry, Ray," I whisper to myself.

Out of the corner of my eye, I see my mom. Oh, wonderful. "Hey, I figured I'd find you here," she says, sitting beside me. I continue staring straight.

"Honey, talk to me. What's wrong?" she asks.

I sigh in frustration. "Both of my dads are dead, Mom." A lump in my throat forms as I hold back tears. "A year apart, I don't understand what I did to deserve this." Before I can continue speaking, I burst into tears. She wraps her arms around me, and I feel like a little kid again, crying over a broken toy, but I just let it out.

"Oh, honey, I'm so sorry. But you didn't do anything to deserve this. No one 'deserves' this." Her voice cracks. "I wish I could press a button and make it better."

I sit up and look at her. A tear falls from her eye. "Mom, when Ray died, I was okay within a few months. Why is this death making it harder for me?"

"I don't know, honey, but maybe it's something you can't work out on your own. Maybe you need help so you can heal."

"Like what?" I scoff. "Therapy at Dr. Ashlyn Kale's?"

She shrugs her shoulders. "Only one way to find out, sweetpea."

I look down, fumbling with my thumbs, and let out a heavy sigh. "We got into a fight, Eric and I."

"About what?"

"I don't even know, Mom. It was stupid."

"Well, if I know anything about love, that man loves you, just like Ray loved me. Despite any argument and rough patch, you will get through it together."

All I do is nod. I didn't have much else to say. I didn't even expect Mom to be out here.

"Let me see that ring," she says, taking my hand. Her eyes widen, and she gasps, running her thumb over the band. "Oh, he did wonderful."

Memories of the argument with Eric linger in my mind. I replay the heated words and the cold silence that followed. It was all so trivial, yet it felt like the foundation of our relationship was shaking. Mom's reassurance offers a glimmer of hope, but the doubt still lingers. Maybe therapy is the answer, maybe not. But I shouldn't ignore it.

"I'm scared," I admit to Eric as we sit in the waiting room of Dr. Kale's office.

"You're going to be okay, I promise," he assures, tenderly kissing the back of my hand.

A woman who looks to be in her mid-thirties enters the waiting room, glancing around. "Ms. Scott?" she inquires.

I stand. "That's me."

"She's ready for you."

I look at Eric, giving him a small smile.

"You've got this," he says. I nod.

Entering the office, I find two inviting dark brown leather chairs flanking a stylish glass coffee table. And there sits Dr. Ashlyn Kale, her curly blond hair gracefully framing her shoulders. Her reassuring smile instantly puts me at ease. She gestures for me to take a seat, so I settle into one of the leather chairs.

"Hi, Hailey, I'm Dr. Ashlyn Kale. but you may call me Ashlyn."

"Hi," I whisper.

"So what would you like to talk about?" she asks.

I shrug. "Honestly, a lot. But I'm not sure where to start."

I wish my life was better, but I don't know how to explain that.

"Well, how about we start with that ring of yours?" she asks, pointing at my hand.

"Oh, um..." I fumble with it. "I got engaged nearly a month ago." I trace the edge of the engagement ring with my fingertips, a nervous habit that's developed over the past month.

"Yeah? Is that the guy out there in the waiting room?"

"Yes, his name's Eric." I smile.

"You seem happy when you mention his name," she states.

"I am. He's been nothing but amazing to

me."

"Where did he propose to you?"

"Hawaii."

"That must have been an incredible moment in Hawaii," she remarks, and a fleeting image of the picturesque proposal dances in my mind. The sun setting, the waves crashing—it was perfect. However, the enchantment of that day is soon overshadowed by the sorrow of the next.

"It was"—I let out a shaky sigh—"until it wasn't."

"What happened?"

"We were supposed to be enjoying the island together," I say, my voice slightly faltering. "You know, just revel in the joy of our engagement. But... something happened. Something I didn't expect."

"What was it?"

I look down. "I received a call from my mom right after our engagement. It was about my dad. He... he had passed away.

"I ran myself to the hotel bathroom," I continue, my voice taking on a more fragile tone. "Locked myself in, undressed, and got in the tub, allowing it to fill, hoping the sound of the water would drown out my cries."

"That must've been hard on you," she says calmly. "How did Eric react?"

I look up at her. "Um, he got into the bathroom somehow, after a while of letting me be alone, and climbed into the tub with me and held me."

"Sounds like he truly cares about you."

"He does, but sometimes I doubt it."

She leans forward. "Doubt it? Why would you doubt his feelings for you?"

"I've always felt that way about the people in my life... I guess I don't really feel worthy enough to be truly loved and cared for."

She pauses. "Communication is key in times like these. Have you talked to him about how you feel?"

I glance away, a mix of guilt and hesitation washing over me. "Not really. I've been afraid to push him away."

She reaches out, placing a comforting hand on mine. "You deserve someone who can handle all aspects of you, especially during the difficult times. Opening up might bring you closer instead of pushing him away."

A tear rolls down my cheek. "I think I'm done for today." I say and stand.

She follows. "How about you come back Saturday, say eleven?"

"Sure." I nod and walk out of the office.

I sit on the couch at home, the room bathed in the soft glow of the TV. It's nighttime, and I'm munching on the spaghetti Eric made for dinner. The TV show plays in the background, its storyline a distraction from my real-world complexities.

I glance over at the kitchen, where Eric is cleaning up, the clinking of dishes echoing in the background. He's already finished his plate, but I've not finished mine. It's like our argument didn't even happen the other day.

"I'm sorry," I say. He looks over at me with a smile.

"About what?"

"Being moody and rude toward you."

He puts the hand towel on the counter and walks over to me.

"Are you done with your food?" he asks, pointing at it.

I nod. He takes it and pats me on the knee before walking back into the kitchen.

CHAPTER FOURTEEN

"Ouch!" I yell. *Fuck, that hurt.* I don't straighten my hair often, but I wanted to look really cute today. Besides, Eric hasn't seen me with straight hair yet.

"Come on, we gotta go!" Scarlett hollers.

"If you had curly hair, you wouldn't be rushing me!" This girl, I swear.

"That's probably true, but we have to be at the bridal shop in thirty minutes."

"Oh, then can you help find me an outfit while I'm getting ready over here?"

She sighs. "Already on it, girlfriend!"

"Don't forget, we also have game night tonight!" I yell.

"Uh, did you forget I'm the one who came up with it?"

"Um, no, because we both came up with it."

"Oh yeah...I'm going to play some music!"

she says.

I roll my eyes, shaking my head with a smile. I finish straightening my hair and grab my makeup bag and notice my lip balm is missing.

"Scar, do you have my lip balm?" I yell out in frustration.

"You left it in the car."

Oh. I do not do well under pressure. I forgot we had just gotten back home from grabbing lunch, and I had put some on in the car. I finish putting my mascara on.

"So this blouse or the white tank top and denim jacket?" she asks, holding them out.

"Second option." I grab the shirts from her and get dressed.

"Probably best to wear leggings today. It'll be easier when you have to take them off and on at the bridal shop," she says, handing me a pair.

"What would I do without you?" I joke.

"Die probably."

I scoff. "No, I wouldn't."

After an hour of trying on dresses, I step up on the small circular platform.

"Oh, that's a pretty dress," my mom and Scarlett say at the same time.

I look in the mirror, smiling at my reflection. The dress hugs my figure just right, and the soft, off-white color compliments my complexion. Scarlett and my mom exchange glances, giving their approval.

"I knew this would be the one." Scarlett grins.

"Absolutely stunning, sweetheart," my mom adds.

After finding the perfect dress, we head to the counter to make the purchase. The sales associate packages it carefully, and I can't resist peeking at it one more time.

"Game night will be so much fun," Scarlett chimes in as we leave the bridal shop.

"You better believe it. I've been looking forward to it all week," I reply.

"Long week, I assume?" Mom asks.

"Yeah, and tomorrow I have another therapy session."

"Hey, Mom, can you take the dress back to your house?" I ask.

"Sure thing."

I walk into the house and catch a strong whiff of lavender, and I can hear water running. I look down and see Eric's boots next to the front door and smile.

"Eric?" I call out. He steps out of the bathroom as I place the car keys on the counter.

"You weren't supposed to be home until later," he says, walking over to me.

"Yeah, but I really wanted to relax before I went to the café," I say, wrapping my arms around his neck.

"Well, I was going to surprise you with this bath later, but I wanted to try the new lavender bubbles first."

I laugh. "Oh really, just to try?"

He raises his hands. "Fine, you caught me. I really wanted a bath with them." He smacks my butt playfully. "Mmm, well... the tub is big enough for us both, you know?"

"I like where you're going with this." He gives me a kiss on the neck and lifts me up by my thighs. I wrap my legs around his waist, squealing and laughing.

I love this man so much.

It's about thirty minutes before everyone piles in here for game night. I wasn't supposed to be at work all week, but Scarlett knows me. She knows taking off all week wasn't the greatest idea.

"Come on, Scarlett, I can't sit at home moping. I gotta move. I've gotta get through this," I plead, looking at her with my brows raised.

"Okay, fine, but you're setting up tables on game night."

"Deal!"

Now here I am, setting up the tables as promised. I place five games per table and set up the scoreboard. Instead of tracking it on paper, we are setting up a board this time for everyone to see. This time, it's going to be a little different.

Country music plays softly in the background, and I can't help but sing along. I may like pop music, but I grew up on country. All the early 2000s are my favorite, from George Strait to Kenny Chesney. A loud boom echoes through the sky. There's that storm. Game night always has to have a storm, small or big.

"Hi, would you like anything to drink?" I ask one of the customers who sits down with two children.

"Hey, yeah, can I get a large caramel cappuccino, and they'll have an apple juice?"

"Sure thing, anything to eat?"

"Umm… do you have any chocolate muffins left?" she asks.

"I sure do. How many?"

"Three."

"Coming right up," I say as I write down her order. I pin the note to the board behind the counter and get to it.

"Hails, you forgot to buy chalk," Scarlett says, walking up to me. *Shit.*

"I didn't forget to buy them. They're at the house."

She sighs. "Well, you forgot to bring them."

"I'm sorry, I'll call Eric and ask if he can bring them by," I say and grab my phone from my pocket, unlocking it and tapping call on Eric's name.

"Hey babe, what's up?" I can hear the tiredness in his voice.

"Hey, baby, can you bring the chalk on your way in? They're on the counter by the microwave," I ask.

"Yes, I'll be right there."

While I'm waiting for Eric to bring the chalk, I focus on getting the tables ready for game night. The rain taps on the windows, adding rhythm perfectly to the background music. The customer with the two children seems content as I bring over their drinks and chocolate muffins.

The air in the café is filled with the aroma of freshly brewed coffee and the sweet scent of muffins, my favorite. About ten minutes go by, and Eric arrives just in time, bringing the much-needed chalk for the scoreboard. I thank him with a quick kiss and immediately start writing the names of the games and the players on the board. The vibrant chalk stands out against the blackboard.

"Okay, everyone, listen up!" Scarlett hollers from where she stands on a table. Everyone turns their heads toward her.

"Once this timer goes off, you may begin your game. We have added something new! If you finish a game, you must hit the bell one time. If you finish all games, you must hit the bell two times!" she says and points at the scoreboard.

"This scoreboard will show us what table is in the lead to help keep track of everyone and where they're at. The prize tonight is tickets to the fishing race across town at my dad's boathouse!" Everyone cheers.

"Enjoy your food and drinks, and begin as soon as this clock dings!"

The storm outside intensifies, but it only heightens the excitement inside. Laughter, the clatter of board game pieces, and the occasional thunderclap are heard throughout the night.

Game night progresses, and the

competition becomes fierce. The scoreboard serves its purpose, keeping everyone engaged and invested in the games. Scarlett and I exchange knowing glances, silently acknowledging tonight will be our most successful game night.

Scarlett raises an eyebrow, a mischievous twinkle in her eyes. "So June twelfth, huh?"

I look at her, a soft smile playing on my lips as I think about the significance behind the chosen date. "I wanted to honor Ray's birthday and memory and have a day that makes me feel more like he's there."

"That's beautiful, Hailey. It's going to be even more of a special day, then."

I sigh and think about how I don't even have a dad to walk me down the aisle.

"Yeah, but I'll be walking myself down the aisle. Such a loner, right?" I joke.

"Oh no, honey, I'll see if Zack will do it."

"What? I barely know him."

"I mean, he's buddies with Eric. Think about it."

In the quiet moments of reflection, I find myself standing at a crossroads, contemplating whether the notion isn't all that bad or if I should tread the path alone. Even if my biological father were still a part of my life, the thought of him walking with me doesn't sit right. He never earned that privilege, unlike Ray.

From my earliest childhood memories, the one constant yearning was for the comforting presence of my daddy. As the pages of time turned, I gradually built a protective shield around that yearning, numbing myself to the once-pervasive desire.

Life, however, has a way of stirring dormant emotions. Whenever a memory of him resurfaces or a situation triggers a profound feeling, the yearning for my daddy resurfaces.

The pain is profound. Each recollection of him leaves me emotionally bruised, prompting relentless questioning of my own worthiness.

Why wasn't I enough for him to envelop me in the love and care a daughter deserves? These kinds of unanswered questions really mess with my head and make me feel all sorts of emotions. And so, I stand at the crossroads, grappling with the complexity of emotions and the choices that lie ahead.

A bell chimes three times, and I've realized I've not been keeping track of the scoreboard. I hurry and grab a piece of chalk, only to see Scarlett already marking things down. Well, now I feel bad for not paying attention.

"We have a game night winner!" Scarlett hollers, arms raised triumphantly in the air. It is the customer with two children from earlier in the evening. I smile, grab the tickets for the fishing race, walk up to her, and hand them over.

"Congrats!" I say.

"Thank you so much! My husband is going to be so excited!" she says.

"Enjoy them! Have fun!" Scarlett says.

The lady walks out with her two kids. The night begins to simmer down, and customers leave within the next hour. I really don't want to go out in the rain.

CHAPTER FIFTEEN

I walk up the stairs of my therapist's office, and the birds chirping this morning make me smile. It's my second time in therapy, but despite my past hesitation and not feeling like it's what I need, I'm glad I'm here.

I check in at the front and take a seat in the waiting room. I'm not sure what the outcome of today's session will be, nor do I know what will be talked about, but I'm ready for whatever today brings. Even though I am awkward when discussing my own feelings, this doctor makes me feel more at ease with them.

At least our first session felt that way. I did sort of rush out, but I was overwhelmed by having to speak to a stranger about everything and sit with my feelings while she took notes.

"Ms. Scott?" her assistant asks.

"Yeah?"

"She's ready for you."

I nod and stand from the chair, following

her to the back and into Dr. Ashlyn's office.

"Hi, Hailey. Please, sit." She gestures.

I do so and cross my left leg over the other.

The room smells like vanilla. Last time, it smelled like lavender. Odd change.

"How have you been since we last spoke?" she asks.

The crinkle in her nose she makes when asking me makes me wonder if she actually cares about her patients. *I need to stop thinking the worst of people.*

"Okay, I guess. I finally got a wedding dress and had a nice time during game night," I say, fumbling with my thumbs. I can't bring myself to talk about anything deeper than basic things about my life.

"Wedding dress? What does it look like?"

"Umm, it's a ball gown. It has these pretty little intricate floral patterns, with sleeves, and no train."

"That sounds lovely," she says, clasping her hands together. "Anything, in particular, you'd like to talk about?"

I purse my lips to the side, not sure how to respond. "I'm not sure really, but lately, I've been more aware of my feelings."

"What kind of feelings?"

I pause, trying to collect my thoughts. The last thing I want is to sound like a babble mouth. "Self doubts, self-worth, insecurities, you know?"

She nods. "I understand. I've been there myself."

"You have?" I ask.

"Yeah, and I'll be honest with you, I still have my moments, but for a long time years ago, I struggled with those pretty much daily."

A therapist who has deep-rooted issues. Perfect.

"I'm not sure when it started, but I sometimes wonder if it's because of the way my dad would treat me," I whisper, my voice cracking.

"In what way would he treat you?"

Breaking her gaze and looking down, I let out a heavy sigh. I'm unable to speak.

"It's okay. We can discuss it later if you'd prefer?"

"No, uh, I've never been asked that question before."

"Not by anyone? Friends? Family?" she asks.

I shake my head. "They already knew everything. They've witnessed it, so there's no need to ask."

"I see." She grabs her notebook and begins jotting down something.

"It was like a cycle with him. You know?

For a few months, everything was fine. We got along great with no issues. But sometimes he'd drunk text me and make me feel like utter shit." I pause, taking a breather. I can go on and on about him and not think twice about what I want to say.

Slut

Cunt

Dumb

Bitch

Stupid

I've been called every name in the book, out of nowhere, and sometimes he wasn't even drunk when it happened.

"And how do you know when he's drunk and when he's not?"

"The time of day he'd text me, or if I called him, I could hear it in his voice. He'd slur his words when he was intoxicated."

"That must have been hard on you," she says.

It was, I guess. But I don't know how to explain how I just pushed it to the side and kept up with my daily tasks without trying to think about it.

"Yeah, it was." That's all I could get out.

It's been a couple of hours now since the therapy session with Dr. Ashlyn Kale. I don't really have much to do today, but just as I look up from my phone, I see the dirty clothes filling the hamper. Looking down and sighing, I lock my phone and place it on the coffee table in front of me and stand. I grab the hamper and head into the laundry room to throw a load in the washer.

I don't really use fragrant laundry stuff as it's caused me skin issues before. I close the washer door and turn it on, and walk back into the living room. God, I didn't realize how much of a mess it was.

I grab a trash bag and pick up the soda cans and food from the table. I take the trash outside and throw it into the garbage can. Right before I get to the kitchen to grab a drink, my phone begins to buzz. Letting out a heavy sigh I grab it, caller ID showing the local hospital. *Hm. That's weird.* My hands shake as I tap the answer button.

"Hello?" I answer.

"Hi, is this Hailey Scott?" A man's voice is heard through the phone.

"This is she."

"I'm calling because you are the first emergency contact on Eric Carter's list. I'm afraid he's been in a car accident."

Panic sets in, and I can feel the adrenaline coursing through my veins. Without a second thought, I cry, "I'm on my way!" I hang up the phone, my hands trembling as I fumble to grab my keys from the table. I rush out the door, the warm afternoon air hitting me as I sprint to my Jeep parked outside.

In a whirlwind of emotions, I start the engine and speed toward the hospital. Thoughts of the accident, of Eric's well-being, and the uncertainty of the situation race through my mind. The normally familiar streets become a blur as I navigate through traffic. My only concern is reaching the hospital as quickly as possible.

As I pull into the hospital parking lot, I spot the emergency sign and hastily park the Jeep. I take a deep breath, trying to steady myself before entering the hospital. The automatic doors slide open, and I step inside.

The receptionist directs me to the emergency room, where I find a nurse who informs me Eric is in surgery. I'm led to a waiting area, the minutes ticking by agonizingly slow as I sit. My leg shakes as I anxiously wait.

I close my eyes, silently hoping for the best while bracing myself for whatever news awaits me about his condition.

Time seems to stretch endlessly as I sit there. The minutes turn into hours, each passing second intensifying the worry gnawing at my insides.

Finally, a doctor approaches me, clad in

scrubs with a weary expression. I stand, my heart pounding and my breath catching in my throat.

"How is he?" I manage to utter, my voice barely above a whisper.

The doctor offers a reassuring smile. "He's out of surgery. He has a badly broken arm, and the procedure went as well as we could hope for, given the circumstances. He's stable now, but it's going to be a long road to recovery. We'll be monitoring him closely."

Relief washes over me, and the doctor leads me through the hallway of the hospital until we reach the room where Eric is recovering.

When I step inside, the sight of him hooked up to machines and monitors tugs at my heart. His eyes flutter open as I approach, a weak but genuine smile playing on his lips. "Hey," he rasps, his voice strained.

"Hi, honey," I say, pulling a chair close to his bedside and sitting down. Tears begin to form, but I blink them away before they fall.

"Don't cry, I'm okay," he says, lifting his arm to caress my cheek.

"I can't help it. I've already lost two people in the span of a year. I can't lose you too," I say and kiss the palm of his hand.

His grip on my hand tightens, and he offers a reassuring squeeze. The sterile scent of the hospital room is overwhelming.

"Do you want me to call your mom?" I ask.

He shakes his head. "No, she's in another state. I don't want her to worry," he says.

With a nod, I hold his hand and watch his face as he closes his eyes, falling asleep.

My heart about ripped out of my chest when I heard he was in the hospital. The way my soul nearly left my body is hard to explain. When both of my dads died, my heart dropped to the pit of my stomach, but this felt deeper and much more heart-wrenching, and Eric's not even gone from this world.

I'm unable to miss another shift at work, and while Eric is recovering from his accident and surgery, I'm here at the café making sure my sanity and paychecks are set in place.

"Eric's in the hospital," I say.

"What? Is he okay?" Scarlett asks me while I'm wiping down the hot coffee I spilled over the counter.

"He's okay. Just hanging in there," I say.

"What happened?"

"He broke his arm."

"Oh, yikes... How did this happen?"

"Some idiot ran a red light, and Eric got hit

while he was crossing the street. It all happened so fast; one moment, he was walking, and the next, he was on the ground with a broken arm. It's infuriating how someone's carelessness can change everything in an instant."

Scarlett's eyes widen with concern. "That's terrible. Will he be okay?"

I take a deep breath, trying to compose myself. "The doctors said he should have a full recovery, but it'll take time."

She nods. "Poor guy. And you, Hails? How are you holding up through all of this?"

I manage a weak smile. "I'm hanging in there. It's just tough, you know? Balancing work, worrying about Eric, dealing with the death of my dad, and trying to keep everything together. But I have to keep going."

Scarlett reaches across the counter to give my hand a reassuring squeeze. "You're strong, Hails. If there's anything I can do to help, just let me know."

"Thank you." I return the squeeze, grateful for the support. "I just hope Eric gets better soon. I hate seeing him like this."

"He's a trouper. He'll get through this."

I hope so, sooner than later.

"By the way, I have an appointment at one with Dr. Kale," I say.

"Do you need the day off?"

"No, I'll come back after I'm done."

I'm sitting on my porch, sipping coffee. I take a moment to look up at the sky. The stars shine brightly without a single cloud, and I can hear the waves from the nearby beach. The air is a mix of ocean freshness and the warmth of my coffee.

It's peaceful, with only the sound of the waves in the background and the trees rustling slightly with the breeze.

Today's not been my day. I nearly tripped up the stairs at the doctor's office and barely ate lunch. I haven't even put dinner together. It seems like ever since Eric has been staying over every night, I'm unable to sleep by myself, so him being in the hospital will make the next couple of nights hard on me.

My phone begins to vibrate, and I take it from my pocket and see Eric FaceTiming me. Speaking of.

I tap answer.

His video is slightly blurry, but I can still see him.

"Hi, baby, miss you," I say.

"I miss you too. Just took some pain meds. I wanted to say good night and I love you before

I sleep." He wipes his eyes.

"Aw, baby, I love you too. I'm going to have a hard time sleeping without you," I confess, the scent of the sea enhancing the emotional connection.

He sighs softly and angles the phone camera more away from his face. "It'll be all right, sweetie. Just two more nights, and I'll be back in bed with you," he reassures me with a soft smile.

My face warms up after he says that.

"Are you outside?"

"Yes, look how pretty these stars are," I say as I switch the camera.

"Wow, those stars are bright."

"I know, no clouds in sight either," I observe, inhaling the scent of the sea breeze deeply.

"Must mean you'll get some good sleep tonight."

"More like you will, with them pain meds in your system." I chuckle, the coffee aroma lingering in the air.

"True. True. Hey, I guess the doctors called my mom. I forgot she was also listed as an emergency contact. She said she's flying in tonight and will be here tomorrow," he shares, and my heart flutters at the news. I've not met his mom yet, but I've heard she's lovely.

"Don't worry, she'll love you." He interrupts

my thoughts.

"I didn't say anything," I protest.

"You didn't have to. I can see the worry on your face." He smiles reassuringly.

I take a breath. "I just want her to like me, that's all."

"Once she meets you, she will."

CHAPTER SIXTEEN

I STAND AT THE COUNTER, WATCHING THE CLOCK TICK BY. We still have twenty minutes before we open. I wish Scarlett would get here soon, but she won't be here until ten this morning. It's a Tuesday, which means I'll be heading to visit Ray straight after work. I can't believe it's been a year since he's been gone. Every time I look over our family photos and selfies we've taken together, I smile happily, but the tug on my heartstrings tries to bring the curves of my lips upside down. As the months have passed, that little quiver of mine subsides almost every time I think of him.

My heart has a hole that will never be filled, as he's not here to keep it intact. Little things I do remind me of him more than they ever did when he was alive.

Every dad joke I say, he's made. Any time I cook, all I can think about are the small funny remarks he'd make about how he's got the fire department on speed dial in case I burn the house down. Any time I order takeout, he'd say, "Oh thank God, I don't have to worry about calling the fire department tonight." He'd give me a hug and follow with, "I love you, daughter. You know I'm just teasing you, sort of." We'd both laugh.

The door's bell chimes, pulling me out of my thoughts. I look up and greet the lady. "Hi, how can I help you today?"

The lady, with a request as straightforward as her demeanor, replies, "Hi, can I get a black coffee with two sugars, please?"

"Certainly. Is there anything else you'd like?" I inquire.

"No, that'll be it," she responds.

I acknowledge her order. "For here or to go?"

"To go, please," she affirms.

"Very well. I'll be right back," I assure her, turning away to retrieve the coffee pitcher. The rich aroma of freshly brewed coffee envelops the air as I carefully pour it into a to-go cup, adding two sugars and ensuring a thorough mix before facing the customer once more.

"That'll be two fifty, please," I state as she hands me her card. With a swift and efficient swipe, the transaction is complete, and I return the card to her.

"Thank you!" she expresses her gratitude, making her way toward the front doors.

"You're welcome!"

Letting out a sigh, I grab my small blue clipboard and begin counting the inventory, as I forgot to do so before my shift began.

Hours go by, and I begin cleaning the dining room as Scarlett handles customers. It's nearly three in the afternoon, and I hurry to finish sweeping so I can take my break. I take the dustpan and throw what I swept into the garbage.

"Hey, Scarlett, I'm heading outside." I take my apron off and place it on the hook.

"Okay, see you after break!"

I grab a blueberry muffin, push open the front doors, and walk out, sitting on the chair we have set up by the front steps. I pull out my phone and unlock it to scroll through social media. I'm not on social media as much as Scarlett is, but I do have them to connect with family and friends mostly. I notice I have a message request from somebody. I tap it open to see one from my uncle, and I didn't even know he had social media.

I read over the message. **I hope you're doing okay, Hailey. I wanted to talk to you about your dad's funeral. I know it must be confusing and hurtful that you weren't invited,**

and I feel the need to explain. It wasn't an easy decision, but your absence was requested by some family members who felt having you there might create additional stress during an already difficult time.

I stare at the screen, my heart sinking. The words echo in my mind. I never thought they saw me that way. The message continues. **They believe your presence could be disruptive, and they wanted to ensure a peaceful and respectful farewell for your father. I know this might be hard to understand, but I wanted to share the reasons behind the decision. If you need someone to talk to or if there's anything I can do, please let me know.**

Tears well up in my eyes as I try to process the words. Excluded from my own father's funeral because they perceive me as an issue. It's a bitter pill to swallow. I take a deep breath, trying to hold back the flood of emotions. The blueberry muffin in my hand suddenly feels tasteless, and the world around me blurs. I never expected to be judged this way by my own family, especially during such a painful moment.

I take another deep breath, trying to hold back the tears threatening to spill over.

I wipe away the single tear that escapes and remove the message from my uncle. The blueberry muffin feels like a heavy weight in my hand. I stand abruptly, tossing the muffin into a nearby trash bin.

As I walk back into the café, I can feel the weight of the emotions settling in the pit of my stomach. The familiar aroma of freshly brewed coffee surrounds me, but it offers little solace. I wash my hands and place my apron on, and fake a smile as I walk up to the counter and try to focus on the rest of my shift.

I pull up to the cemetery and grab my blue blanket from the passenger seat and step out of the car, closing the door behind me. With each step on the soft grass beneath my feet, a lump begins to form in my throat. I open the blanket and place it over the grass and sit down.

I shake uncontrollably, bursting into tears, covering my face with my elbows resting on my knees.

"Why did you have to leave me, Daddy?" I mutter through the tears. Ray is the dad who stepped up and showed me what a father's love really means and what it should be. Which shatters my heart even more thinking about it since his love for me should be unconditional.

It is painful to finally understand the limited support my biological father provided compared to the expectations of what a father's role should be.

My phone begins to buzz, and my fingers tremble as I wipe the tears from my eyes. I reach for my phone and see Eric pop up on my screen.

ERIC

> Hey, sweetie, they are sending me home earlier than expected. Come get me within the hour?

Oh thank God.

ME

> Yes, I'll be there soon.

I put my phone back in my pocket and look over Ray's tombstone.

"I'll be back next Tuesday, as always," I say and stand, taking my blanket and heading back to the car.

CHAPTER SEVENTEEN

WALKING INTO HOSPITALS FEELS LIKE WALKING DIRECTLY into the path of a minefield. Yet I navigate this minefield on my way to Eric's room as if I'm on autopilot. As I open the door, a dark-haired woman catches my eye. She's seated on a chair next to Eric's bedside.

"Hi, babe! This is my mom. Mom, meet Hailey, my fiancée," Eric warmly introduces us.

I offer a nervous smile and extend my hand. "Hi, nice to meet you."

"Oh honey, give me a hug," she invites with a soft, welcoming voice.

"Sure," I agree, sharing a hug with her as I notice Eric winking at me, silently mouthing, "I told you." Rolling my eyes in jest, I release the hug.

"It's nice to meet you, Hailey. Welcome to the family," she says kindly.

"Thank you," I reply, grabbing a chair from the corner and positioning it next to Eric on the other side before taking a seat.

"How are you feeling?" I inquire.

"Better. It'll take about a month or so for me to fully use my arm, so I'll be out of work for a bit," he explains.

Frowning, I sympathize. "I'm sorry, I know how much you enjoy your job."

"On the bright side, I can enjoy uninterrupted daily quality time with you," he adds playfully. My face heats, and I notice his mom smiling as well.

"Mrs. Carter, where are you staying?" I ask.

"Oh, I'm just going to camp out at his apartment for the weekend before heading back home," she answers.

I nod and turn back to Eric. "Have they given you your discharge papers yet?"

"No, still waiting on the doctor."

Waiting to leave the hospital seemed to take an eternity. It took almost two hours to get his discharge papers. With my impatience and the gravity of the situation, I was not the best companion at the moment.

"I love you," I whisper as I cover Eric with a comforter.

"I love you too," he responds, and we share a tender kiss. His hand rests softly on my cheek, his lips forming a gentle smile. I step out of the room, closing the door behind me.

"He's officially resting now," I inform his mother while taking the seat beside her on the couch.

"Your place is lovely, Hailey."

"Thank you. I'll be honest, though. Decorating isn't my forte," I joke.

"Oh, really? You did well with this living room," she compliments as she glances around.

Yeah, thanks to Scarlett. I'll avoid mentioning it wasn't my handiwork.

"Would you like something to drink or eat?" I offer.

"Water is fine, thank you."

I stand, grab a glass, fill it with water, and return to her, handing it over before sitting back down.

"Eric mentioned you like romance books. What author have you read recently?"

"Oh, I recently enjoyed a novel by Nora Roberts."

"Her storytelling has a certain charm," she responds, sipping the water.

"That's great! Nora Roberts is indeed a fantastic author," I reply, relieved to have found a conversational thread.

"Have you read any of her books?"

"I have, I believe it was…" I try to remember the title. "Oh, *Of Blood and Bone.*"

"Was it good? I've been thinking of picking that one up for my next read," she says, taking another sip of her water.

"Definitely do so! It's incredible, and I won't spoil it."

"I'll make sure to add it to my list. There's nothing better than getting lost in an incredible book!"

She stands up from the couch, grabbing her purse with a slight stretch. "Well, I better head to Eric's place. I could really use a shower and some sleep," she says, her tone a mix of weariness and anticipation.

"See you tomorrow, Mrs. Carter." I give her a hug, and she does the same before heading out.

CHAPTER EIGHTEEN

BEEP-BEEP

BEEP-BEEP

BEEP-BEEP

The grating sound of the alarm clock fills the room, prompting me to nudge Eric and reach for the snooze button.

He's been at home for a few weeks, yet the annoying beeps of his nonstop alarm clock persist.

"Babe, I'm honestly about to throw that out the window," I say, throwing the blanket off my legs and standing.

"If I turn it off all month, my routine will mess up."

"I know, I know. Just annoying." Tying my robe around my waist, I put my slippers on.

"You're annoying," he whispers as he places the blanket over his face.

I roll my eyes and step out of my bedroom

and into the kitchen to make coffee. When I hear a knock on the door, I look over at the clock on the stove, and it's not even six yet. Slowly, I walk to my door and look outside my peephole, only to see Scarlett with a tearstained face and dressed in baggy clothes.

I hurry and open the door. "Scarlett, what's wrong?"

She steps inside the house and sits on the barstool in the kitchen. I close the door, locking it behind me and follow her.

"Zack, he cheated on me!"

I gasp, my hand instinctively reaching out to comfort Scarlett.

"I can't believe he would do that to you," I say, placing a comforting hand on her shoulder.

Tears streaming down her face. "You know that one girl who tried starting a fight at his party?"

I nod.

"Well, I went to bring him a surprise lunch when I noticed a car I've not seen before in his driveway, and when I looked up from where I was standing"—she takes a quick breath—"I could see them through his bedroom window, kissing."

"What a fucking asshole," Eric says, walking into the kitchen.

"Please, don't say anything. I haven't confronted him yet."

"Once you do, let me know because his ass is grass when I get ahold of him."

I roll my eyes at Eric's response. "I was going to call you earlier about going bridesmaid dress shopping today, but if you aren't in the mood to, I understand," I say, holding Scarlett's hand.

"I just need a shower, then coffee, and we can head out? I need to take my mind off him," she whispers.

I nod, leading Scarlett to the guest bathroom, where she can freshen up. As she disappears into the bathroom, I exchange a concerned glance with Eric, silently acknowledging the complexity of the situation.

He places a gentle hand on my shoulder, offering silent support. "She's lucky to have you as a friend."

"I'm so nervous," I admit, crossing my arms as Scarlett and I walk into the dress shop. The interior is beautifully decorated with off-white walls, tile floors, and white lights. Yellow roses are thoughtfully placed in nearly every corner, making the area comfortable with a flowery scent.

"For what?"

"My wedding, I feel as if something bad

may happen." I let out a shaky breath.

"Hi, ladies, what may I help you find today?" a woman with a beautiful dark blue blouse and knee-length skirt welcomes us.

"Hi, we're shopping for a bridesmaid dress today," I say.

"Right this way." The woman guides us toward the back of the shop. The number of dresses in here is outstanding and all so beautiful.

"Did you need any help?"

"Not yet, thank you." I smile.

"Just let me know," she says, walking back to the front.

Scarlett looks around, touching every dress. "Ugh, so gorgeous and hard to choose."

"Well, as long as it's a burgundy, you're safe." I grab one from the rack. "How about you try this one? I'll find a few more in the meantime."

She takes the dress, squealing quietly, and enters a dressing room. I look over the dresses. Each one is beautiful. She's my only bridesmaid, so I want her to look as gorgeous as ever.

My phone buzzes, and I take it from my pocket. Eric's name appears.

"Hi, babe, everything okay?" I answer.

"Yes. I just wanted to let you know my

mom plans on coming over later this afternoon to bring us dinner." His voice has a hint of sleepiness to it.

"That's nice of her. What is she bringing?"

"Lasagna."

"Oh, I've not had that in a while."

"Well, she makes a great one!"

"I bet. What time?"

"Around five."

"Okay, I'll be home before then. Love you."

"I love you too."

Placing my phone back into my pocket, I grab one of the other dresses from the rack and walk toward the dressing room, knocking.

Scarlett opens the door, the dress in her hands making her eyes sparkle with excitement. "What do you think?" she asks, twirling around in front of the mirror.

The silky long dress looks beautiful on her. The burgundy shade suits her well.

"It looks stunning on you." I grin, genuinely pleased. "But let's see how it feels. You never know until you try sitting down or dancing a little."

She chuckles. "Good point. I really like the V-neck of this dress." Scarlett carefully sits on the little bench in the dressing room, making sure the dress flows gracefully. "So any updates on your side?"

I pull out my phone, glancing at the time. "Eric's mom is bringing us dinner later, around five. She's making her famous lasagna."

Scarlett's eyes widen. "Lasagna? Yum!"

"Right? Anyway, try on these other dresses. We need to find the perfect one for you," I say, handing her another hanger with a different burgundy dress.

As Scarlett changes, I can't help but reflect on the upcoming wedding. The nerves that had settled in my stomach earlier resurface. I hope everything goes smoothly.

My mind wanders back to the day Eric proposed. The setting sun painted the sky with hues of orange and pink as he got down on one knee. It was perfect, and I want the wedding to be just as magical.

Scarlett steps out in the second dress, and I can tell by the sparkle in her eyes she loves it. It complements her figure, and the rich burgundy color suits her complexion.

"This one's cute!" she says, twirling again.

"Agreed!"

The shop's atmosphere, filled with the excitement of wedding preparations, eases my worries. Maybe I'm just letting the stress get to me.

As Scarlett heads back into the dressing room with another dress, I take a moment to send a quick text to Eric, letting him know about our progress. I need his calming presence, even if it's just through a screen.

The reply comes almost instantly.

ERIC

You're doing great! Love you.

I smile, feeling a warmth spread through me.

Scarlett emerges from the dressing room in a third dress, and we exchange approving glances. A long silk burgundy dress. This one seems to capture the elegance we're aiming for.

"I think we might have a winner." She grins, twirling once more.

"I agree. This one is perfect," I say, relieved to have found a dress that not only complements her but also aligns with my vision for the wedding.

I wait as she changes back into her own clothes.

We gather the chosen dress and head toward the front of the shop to make the purchase. The woman who welcomed us earlier is there, her warm smile making the process even more delightful.

"Find the perfect one?" she asks.

"Yes, we did. Thank you," I reply.

As we leave the bridal shop, bags in hand, Scarlett and I share a lighthearted laugh.

After our shopping spree, we decide to swing by her place before I head back home for dinner. "Want to come up for a bit? I can make us some tea," she offers.

I check the time, realizing I have a bit before heading back to meet Eric and his mom. "Yes!"

We step into the house, and Scarlett heads to the kitchen.

"Where's your cat?" I ask.

"He's with my dad, I couldn't keep up with him anymore, so I asked if he'd care for him."

"Oh, shucks, I liked having my little buddy while here." I frown.

"Yeah, but I had to do what's best for him. So spill the beans. How are you really feeling about the wedding?" Scarlett asks as she prepares the tea.

I sigh, my guard lowering as I lean against

the kitchen counter. "Honestly, I'm a bundle of nerves. What if something goes wrong? What if I'm not cut out for all of this?"

She turns to face me. "You've got this. You and Eric are meant to be together, and your wedding will be beautiful. It's natural to feel a little overwhelmed."

"But I can't help but feel like something may go wrong."

"That's just your nerves talking. Drink the tea and sit for a bit." She hands me a mug, and I head into the living room, Scarlett following close behind, and we sit on the couch.

"I'm excited for you. Eric is such a catch, and you two are perfect together," Scarlett says with a grin.

I chuckle. "Yeah, he's pretty amazing. But I can't shake these nerves. It's like the closer the wedding gets, the more I worry about every little detail."

Scarlett places her tea on the coffee table and leans back into the cushions.

"It's understandable. But trust me, all those worries will vanish once you see Eric waiting for you at the altar. And think about all the people who'll be there to support you. Your family, friends, and even people like me who love you dearly."

I smile, comforted by her words. "You're right. I'm lucky to have so much love around me. And having you as my bridesmaid makes it even more special."

"The honor is all mine. I can't wait to stand by your side on the big day. And speaking of guests, who else is coming? I know Eric's mom will be there."

I lean forward, listing off the attendees. "Well, both our families, of course. My mom, his mom, and some close relatives. Then there are friends, coworkers, and a few old college buddies. Oh, and don't forget Eric's childhood friends. It will be a diverse crowd, but that makes it special, right?"

"It sounds like a wonderful mix of people. And you'll have me by your side, helping with any last-minute jitters."

I playfully roll my eyes. "You better, I might need a calming presence when walking down that aisle."

She reaches for her tea again, taking a sip. "Maybe we should plan a little pre-wedding get-together. A girls' night or something. Just to unwind and enjoy the moments leading up to the big day."

I raise a brow. "That sounds fun. What do you have in mind?"

"I was thinking we could have a bachelorette party at the café on the day it's closed, maybe bring some girls from the college."

I ponder the idea, a smile forming at

Scarlett's suggestion. "A pre-wedding girls' night at the café? That sounds fun."

"You know what would add a hilarious twist?" she says. "We could invite Jake, that hunky fireman from the station."

I burst into laughter. "Oh, the girls would love that! Can you imagine him showing up in his firefighter gear? We might need to have a fire extinguisher nearby!"

She joins in the laughter. "Exactly!"

"Maybe he could give a 'fire safety' demonstration, complete with cheesy pickup lines. You know, 'Is it hot in here, or is it just me?'" I suggest with a playful wink.

"Oh, that's golden! And if things get too wild, he can use his 'firefighter authority' to bring some order to the chaos. It's like having a built-in chaperone with a hose!" She laughs.

A twinge of guilt nags at me. "Hold on a second, Scarlett," I say, my laughter fading as I shift uncomfortably on the couch. "I don't know about this. I mean, Eric is the love of my life and bringing in a handsome firefighter to entertain us... It just feels like I'd be betraying him in some way."

Her expression softens, understanding my concern. "Hailey, it's all in good fun. Jake is just a friend, and it's not like anything inappropriate would happen. It's just a playful addition to the party, like having a celebrity crush or something."

I nod, still feeling conflicted. "I get that, but it's just that Eric is the one I want to be with. I don't want anything or anyone else distracting from that, even in a joking way."

She places a comforting hand on my shoulder. "I understand. We'll come up with something else that's fun but won't make you feel uncomfortable. The last thing we want is for you to have any regrets or doubts about your bachelorette party."

Setting the empty cup down on the coffee table, I glance at the time and realize I need to start heading back home for dinner with Eric and his mom. "Thank you for this."

She smiles warmly. "I love you, girly. I'm here for you through the wedding planning and beyond."

I stand, giving Scarlett a sincere hug. "You're the best."

"I know," she says jokingly.

As I make my way to the door, she walks me out. With a final wave, I step out and head toward my car.

CHAPTER NINETEEN

I walk inside my house and see Eric sitting on the couch. I place my car keys down on the counter, then slip my shoes off and make my way over to sit next to him.

"Hey," I greet him, a curious smile playing on my lips. "What's on your mind?"

"You, as always," he says, placing his good arm over my shoulders.

"Is your mom on the way yet?" I ask.

"Yes, she called about five minutes ago."

"Oh, good, I'm starving and also looking forward to getting to know her more."

"I'm glad you two connected instantly. She's been wanting me to find someone for forever."

"Oh yeah? You've been a loner for a while, or what?"

"Pretty much."

A knock on the door interrupts our

conversation, and I stand. "Looks like that might be her." I walk over to the door and open it, and it's Eric's mom holding a pan of lasagna.

"Hi, come on in." I gesture my hand toward the kitchen, and she makes her way inside.

"Can I just say how much I love your kitchen?" She compliments me, setting the food down on top of the stove.

"Thank you, I'm glad."

"I mean, the island is my favorite. I wish I had it myself," she mentions.

"The island is what sold me on this place."

Eric chuckles from the living room as he overhears our conversation. "The kitchen island has always been a point of contention between us," he admits, smirking. "I've never understood why she loves it so much."

"Well, islands are a nice finish to a home. Let her be." She laughs.

I pull three plates from the cabinet, place them on the counter, then grab a few forks.

"Babe, dinnertime," I say.

"Already in here!" he hollers. *Oh good.*

I grab our plates and walk around the kitchen into the dining room and set them down, his mom following me.

"This looks and smells delicious, Mrs. Carter." I grab a fork and take a bite. "Oh, yes, delicious for sure."

"Why, thank you. Unfortunately, my son here didn't have all the ingredients I needed, so I went out and bought some stuff to make the noodles homemade."

"You'll have to teach me how to make noodles from scratch."

"Sounds like a plan."

As I sit here eating my food, I can't help but notice how much Eric and his mom look alike. They have the same hair color, eyes, nose, and chin. It's incredible. She really seems to be a lovely person.

"Hailey, have you picked out your wedding dress yet?" she asks.

"Yes, I did." I take my phone out of my pocket and unlock it, finding the photo of it to show her.

"I can't wait to see you in it," Eric says.

I can feel the blood rushing into my cheeks, locking eyes with him for a moment before focusing back on the photo.

"Oh, it's breathtaking!" She glances at Eric and me again. "I noticed a treadmill over there in the hall. Do you work out often?"

I nod slowly. "Yeah, I haven't used it for a while because I've been walking outside more lately. Fresh air has been more beneficial for me these days." I shrug, stealing a glance at Eric.

"That's good. That way, you can fit into

your dress more comfortably," she remarks casually.

I nearly spit out the food I'm chewing.

"Mom!" Eric shouts, placing his fork on the table.

"What?" She looks at him. "I mean, isn't that why you're working out?" She turns to face me.

"Excuse me," I say, grabbing my plate and walking into the kitchen. I toss what's left away and place the dirty dish in the sink before stepping outside into my backyard.

What. The. Fuck.

She said the words so innocently, like she didn't know she was asking such a rude question. She doesn't seem so nice now. I look up at the dark sky as I sit out on my back patio, no porch light or anything on. The only light shining is the moonlight casting a beautiful subtle glow, enough to make me feel somewhat at ease.

"Hailey?" I hear Eric's voice behind me.

"I'm fine." I lie straight through my teeth.

"Bullshit, I know you're not." He closes the screen door and sits down beside me.

I shrug, and he wraps his good arm around

me, a sigh escaping his lips.

"I have no idea why she said that. I'm so sorry."

A tear escapes my eye and falls down my cheek, and I reach to wipe it away as quickly as possible.

"It's okay, really. I'm just going to call it a night." I look at him. "Please don't worry."

"No, I will worry. It was uncalled for, and you are the love of my life. I won't allow such comments toward you." He squeezes my shoulder and side hugs me close. "I made her leave. I will be going to my place before noon tomorrow and settling it."

"I don't want to cause more issues. Maybe she didn't mean it like that."

"Whether she meant it in a bad way or not, it's still not something you say to someone."

I nod. "Let's head to bed?"

"Yes."

I stand, as does he, and we walk back inside the house. I look at the clock. It's only eight, and I already want to end the night. I sigh, change into my blue nightgown, and lie in bed as Eric does the same. "Come here," he says, gesturing for me to lay my head on his chest. He pulls the blanket farther over us, and I fall asleep to the beat of his heart.

Tuesday rolls around. It's been a couple of days since his mother made those comments. I haven't really wanted to face her since then, and Eric has been considerate, but I can tell he's hurt by the situation. I understand his point of view. The two people he loves so dearly aren't exactly on the right track, and that's not okay, but unless she comes to me, I don't exactly feel up to facing her on my own.

I haven't spoken to my mom since we went wedding dress shopping. I need to pick her up after work today so we can head to the cemetery together.

"What the shit!" Scarlett yells out as she comes through the hallway from the back of the café.

"What?" I jump.

"That bitch is on his Instagram!" she screams, looking at me and back at her phone.

"All right, all right, calm down. We are at work, girly." I walk over to her and take a look at her phone screen to see a photo of him and the girl kissing.

"Why would he post this? Have you talked to him yet?" I ask.

"Yes, we broke up once you left my house yesterday."

"I'm so sorry, babe." I give her a hug. "Movie night tomorrow night?" I ask.

"Yes, please."

CHAPTER TWENTY

I rub my chest as Mom and I walk up to Ray's tombstone. One look at her face, and I'm already on the verge of tears. I come out here mostly by myself.

"He would be so proud of you," she says softly, placing her arm over my back in comfort.

"I miss him so much, Mom." I long to reach out for a hug from him, being held by the one person who raised me to understand how a father's love should be. I need that right now.

I lay out the blue blanket. I chose Tuesday because it's the day after they cut the grass, and it feels refreshing and more relaxing under these circumstances. Every breath I take becomes more shaky, and a lump forms in my throat.

"How come you've not been coming out here as much?" I ask, sitting down on the blanket, Mom doing the same.

"Well, every time I do, I bawl my eyes out,

and I need to allow myself some space before coming back."

"And that's why you've been dodging my invitation to come out here?"

"Yes. I'm sorry, darlin'."

"Mom, I want you to know I love you, and you're not alone," I say, gently resting my head on her shoulder. She reciprocates by leaning her head on mine, and we gaze at his tombstone in silence. A lone tear escapes my eye, tracing a path down my cheek. Memories flood my mind, especially those moments when he used to wait for me after school, his weathered Chevy standing out among the posh cars of the affluent soccer moms. Despite the judgmental glares, we never cared. In fact, we used to treat ourselves to some french fries, mocking the disdainful looks we received. We found comfort in our shared understanding these people were stuck-up, and we appreciated the value of money more than they did, acknowledging how fortunate they were, even if they didn't realize it.

"I met his mom, by the way," I blurt out to break the sad silence that has embraced us.

She leans to sit back up, looking straight at me. "What is she like?"

Should I be honest or flat-out lie? "She was lovely, at first," I admit.

"Was?" Her lips curl, and her eyes widen.

"Yes, she was nice until she made a snide comment during dinner the other night."

"What kind of snide comment?" she asks.

"Well, she brought over dinner the other night and ended up saying some things about my weight once she saw my treadmill and my wedding dress."

"What the hell? Oh no, let me see that bitch and tell her to say it to my face!" Her lips press into a tight, flat line before she stands.

"Mom, Eric is handling it, I promise."

"I don't care. This momma bear has officially kicked in!" She grabs her purse from the ground. I stand with her, fold my blanket and follow her to my car.

I grab her arm, making her face me. "Mom! Please don't. I don't want things to get worse, please?" I beg. "Just let Eric handle it. It's his responsibility to do so."

She looks at me, her eyes softening. "Okay, okay, but if there's a next time, I'm getting involved." I let go, and she settles in the car.

I return home from spending time with my mom and walk in the house only to find Eric making a smoothie.

"Hi, babe!" He greets me with a kiss.

"Hi, what kind of smoothie are you making?" I ask.

"Well, I'm making myself a blueberry smoothie. Did you want one?"

"Yes!" I open the freezer, pull out my frozen strawberries and bananas, and place them on the island.

"Do you want me to help?" I ask, eyeballing his arm.

"I still have one arm," he jokes with a grin.

"Okay, whatever you say." I laugh. "I'm going to shower," I say and walk into the bathroom. I undress and pull out two towels from the closet; one for my body and one for my hair.

Turning on the shower, I wait until the water heats, then step in.

The warm water falls onto my shoulders, relaxing the tension, making me tilt my head back and seeking more of the comfort it brings.

I hear the bathroom door open and shut. "Got room for one more?"

"Yes, I do."

I hear him cover his cast before dropping his clothes. A warmth spreads through my cheeks as he steps into my small shower, our bodies not having much choice but to press against one another.

His fingertips glide down my arm, causing my body to erupt into goosebumps. I turn to face him, and he presses his lips against my neck, leaving trails of kisses leading up to the edge of my chin and to my lips. He hovers over them gently.

"I love you," he whispers. He takes my wrist with his good arm and lifts my arm above my head, leaning It against the shower wall behind me.

"Keep It there,"

My heart pounds through my chest as he takes his hand and grabs my ass cheek. I close my eyes from the fluttering sensations in my chest, and he leans down to lick my right nipple slowly. A moan escapes my lips, and I can feel myself becoming wet and more sensitive.

I push my hands forward and wrap my arms around his neck. I look up into his blue eyes. His pupils are dilated, and I can feel my eyes water as I stare into his.

"Fuck me." I beg for his touch, my entire being craving more from him.

"Excuse me?" he asks with a smirk dancing on the curve of his mouth.

"I said fuck me!"

He growls and turns me around, making me face the shower wall. He takes his hands and grips my hips slightly rough, leaning in. "Ask me that again." His voice is deep and oh-so sexy.

"Please fuck me, Eric." A heavy sigh comes

through as I look up at him, hot water flowing over our already heated bodies. He reaches down and turns the water off, opening the curtain and stepping out.

He gives me my towel. I don't even care about my hair being soaked at this point. We dry off as much and as quickly as possible, and he throws his towel on the floor, and I do the same. He lifts me into his arms, and my eyes widen as he does so with just one arm. And I wrap my legs around his waist. He opens the bathroom door leading us into the bedroom as he kisses me.

He lays me down on the bed and pulls away, kissing down my neck and chest. My heart races as he reaches the top of my lips, his tongue slowly teasing around the insides of them and flicking gently on my clit.

I jolt as he does so. He goes faster, and between kissing and licking, he sucks, making me squirm. My toes curl, and I grip the sheets with my fists. He slowly stops, and I whine.

"Oh, you wanted more, huh?"

I nod.

"Too bad, you asked to be fucked, and here I am." He takes his hard cock and slowly slides inside me, and I roll my eyes back in pleasure. A warming sensation comes through, and a loud moan escapes my lips as he picks up the pace. "Oh my God, yes!" I couldn't help myself. I grip the sheets as my body shakes from the sudden flush of warmth spreading through my lower half, shuddering as he groans. "Oh fuck yes, clench on me, baby!" he yells out, tipping his head back as his throbbing cock finishes inside me before slipping out.

"You amaze me," he says, hovering over to kiss me.

CHAPTER TWENTY ONE

Between the madness of my approaching wedding and the shocking end of Scarlett's relationship, we both need a day to just relax. No wedding planning. No family drama. Nothing.

Just two best friends enjoying a day at the beach and a movie night together.

"I'm so glad we're doing this. I need to get out of my own head and have some fun," Scarlett says as we walk across the warm sand on a quieter area of the beach.

The water ahead of us rolls and crashes against the shoreline in subtle waves, foam bubbling on the wet sand. The smells of salt and sun fill my nose, helping my tense shoulders relax as we pick a spot to lay down our towels.

"I'm right there with you," I reply as I fluff out my beach towel before taking a seat.

Scarlett digs around in her beach bag, pulling out the to-go turkey sandwiches, potato chips, and bottles of water we picked up from the store down the street. "I'm starving to death!" she mutters as she unwraps her sandwich.

"Don't fill up too much. We've got a night full of scary movies, pizza, and ice cream ahead of us," I warn her as I offer her a smile.

Scarlett gives me a look of awe as she nudges my knee. "You really are the best. Who needs a cheating ex-boyfriend when I have the best friend in the world?"

An ache hits me in the chest when I remember the tears streaming down her anguished face when she told me about Zack. No one wants to see their best friend heartbroken, and I hate this happened so close to my wedding. I hope it isn't salt in her open wound.

"Forget Zack. He's not even worth the thought. We're going to get tan and stuff ourselves with all the food we love," I say as I tilt my bottle of water toward her.

"Hell yes!" Scarlett quips before tapping her bottle against mine.

We devour our sandwiches and chips, enjoying the soft ocean breeze and the comforting warmth of the sun above us. After stripping down to our swimsuits and putting on sunscreen, we relax and lay on our towels, our sunglasses blocking the sun rays.

This feels like paradise. Even if it's only temporary.

Despite trying to relax, my mind races, bouncing from topic to topic.

Eric's mom.

The wedding.

The future.

Life is moving so quickly, but that's okay because I'm happy.

A little stressed but happy. Then again, who isn't stressed before their wedding? This is the biggest celebration I'll ever have in my entire life, and I just want it to be perfect.

"You should spend the night," I say, breaking the comfortable silence that settled between us.

"You sure?" Scarlett asks as she turns her head to peer at me.

I nod as I smile at her. We see each other at work a lot, but hanging out at work is way different from hanging out outside of work. "Of course! Things are about to get so crazy."

"You're about to be a married woman. You'll be plenty busy," Scarlett replies, flashing me a teasing smile.

I roll my eyes and nudge her arm. After the wedding, what will come next? People are expected to hit certain milestones at specific times in their lives. Marriage. A house. Kids. All of it is a whirlwind in my head, making my chest grow tight with nervousness.

But the moment I think about Eric, the tension fades away like ice under the hot sun. Life is uncertain, and surprises await us around every corner. But at least I'm not alone.

Eric will be by my side no matter what, and our wedding will be as close to perfect as it can be.

Eventually, we start to get a little overheated, and our skin starts to slightly burn. We gather our things and hurry to the car. On the way there, I call in a delivery order for a large supreme pizza, and my stomach threatens to rumble just at the thought.

Something about being at the beach makes me feel like I'm starving.

"I'll pick the movie! You get the snacks!" Scarlett calls out once we walk into the house. She makes a beeline to the living room to browse around on Netflix while I venture into the kitchen with an amused look on my face.

Moments like these remind me of my youth. Even if adulthood is crazy and complicated, there are still moments when life is so sweet, like movie nights with Scarlett, shopping with my mom, or cuddling in bed with Eric.

"You better pick a good one," I tease her, grabbing two cans of soda and a few other snacks before heading to the living room.

Scarlett has already sunk into the couch cushion with her feet curled up next to her. She filters through all the movies before gasping and selecting one of the older horror movies. "This is a classic!"

"Good choice," I say as I place everything on the coffee table. The doorbell ringing sends me hurrying back to the foyer to grab our pizza, which nearly burns my hand through the cardboard box because it's still so hot.

"That smells heavenly," Scarlett gasps when I open the box, revealing a cheesy, piping-hot masterpiece adorned with all sorts of toppings.

I don't say anything because my mouth is watering now. We each grab a slice with a napkin and officially kick off our movie night as the opening credits play on the flat-screen television.

"What's Eric up to?" Scarlett asks before taking a bite of her pizza. She winces at the heat but continues eating, driven by her hunger more than her pain.

"Resting. His arm's almost healed," I tell her.

"That's good," she says.

Scarlett goes quiet for a few minutes, and at first, I think she's sucked into the movie until she sniffles.

"Are you okay?" I ask as a worried look fills my face.

Scarlett scoffs at herself and nods, fanning her face as she rapidly blinks her eyes. She's obviously trying to fight back tears, which makes my heart ache. "Yeah, sorry. Stupid Zack."

I set my half-eaten slice of pizza down and scoot closer to her. She's put up a good front since we first talked about Zack cheating on her, but I can only imagine how much hurt she's been hiding behind her bright smile. "I'm sorry he hurt you. You didn't deserve that."

Scarlett swallows hard and nods, looking far more defeated than I had seen her look in a while.

"I know. It just sucks. I was excited to bring him to the wedding with me, and we even had plans to take a little trip together in a few weeks. I just don't understand how he could make all these plans while also cheating on me with another woman."

"Because he's a jerk!" I exclaim as I place my hand on her shoulder, coaxing her to look me in the eyes. "He wasn't the right guy. The right one will come along."

Scarlett pouts as she takes another bite of pizza, making me smile a little. Even when she's feeling down, she's still her same likable self. No one can take Scarlett's spark away. "Easy for you to say. You found the right guy. You're about to marry him!"

I'm lucky. I feel that way every single day when I think about the loving relationship I have with Eric. It's always felt so natural and right. I can't imagine diving into the dating scene after so long and trying to find someone I can trust and love all over again.

"Hey, don't give up hope. I want to be at your wedding someday too," I tell her.

Scarlett smiles and flips her blond hair behind her shoulder. "All right, I feel motivated."

We share a laugh as the tension fizzles away. Heartbreak is never easy, but I know there's something better for her up ahead. "Just remember you came out of this on top. You're not the one who stooped so low."

And I know all about people who stoop low. An uneasy feeling churns in my stomach as the thought of my dad threatens to break into my mind. *Not now!*

All I want to do is enjoy a fun night with my best friend. The last thing I want to do is think about the people who have hurt me. Besides, he's gone from my life, and I want to focus on who's in my corner now. They're who matter.

Scarlett nods as a determined expression forms on her face. "You're right. I'm better than that."

"A lot of people are coming to the wedding. Who knows who you'll meet?" I raise my eyebrows at her in a playful manner.

Scarlett bursts out laughing. "Look at you! I think my bad influence is rubbing off on you."

"I just know what my best friend needs when she's down," I say as I bump my shoulder against hers. We've known each other for a while now and know what each other needs in our darkest moments.

Scarlett gives me a grateful look that expresses all the thankful words she isn't able to get out. We share one more smile before turning our focus back to the movie as the drama unfolds.

Hopefully, it all stays behind the television screen, but knowing my life, drama always finds its way around to me.

CHAPTER TWENTY TWO

The next few days seem to fly by in a rush until Thursday, but it always seems like the last part of the week drags on agonizingly slow until the weekend. I'm just glad to be keeping myself busy with work and helping Eric out because the moment I let my mind wander, I'm sacked with stressful thoughts.

What can I say? I'm a worrier. An overthinker.

"What are you thinking about?"

I snap out of my thoughts and turn to Eric, who sits on my couch with his broken arm resting on his chest. Of course, he can read me like an open book. "Have you talked to your mom?"

Eric frowns as we're both brought back to that night when she made such an insulting comment about my weight to me. Who does that to a bride right before her wedding? "I haven't heard from her. I've given her every opportunity to come around and apologize after I called her out on her behavior."

I nod and flash him a grateful look. I've heard horror stories about sons always taking their mother's side over their partner's, and I'm glad he's not one of those guys. It stings his mom hasn't apologized yet, but I don't want to linger on that.

"I have to leave for work soon. Make sure you take these," I say as I pick up his pain medication from the coffee table and shake the bottle at him.

Eric takes them and nods. "I will. I hate just sitting around while you go off to work."

I stare at him pointedly. He shouldn't feel guilty at all because none of this is his fault! But I am frustrated the police still haven't found the hit-and-run driver yet. Will Eric ever get justice for having his life thrown off track like this?

It's just not fair so many people get away with bad things. I've seen it happen right in front of my eyes so often.

"You're injured. You need to be taking it easy," I remind him before walking closer so I can peck him on the lips. "Besides, it's supposed to storm tomorrow, so you know what you'll be subjected to."

Eric chuckles. "Game night at the café."

I smile in an amused manner as I nod. Right on the money. With Scarlett being pretty rich and all, tomorrow's winners may actually win a decent amount of money. Her generosity when it comes to prizes typically leads to a packed house on game nights, even when it's raining.

"Text me if you need anything," I tell him, squeezing his hand before gathering my things and heading out of the house.

The commute goes by quickly, especially since it's so early in the morning. When I reach the café, I unlock the door and flip on all the lights, falling into my usual routine of opening the store before Scarlett bursts into the place smelling like her expensive perfume.

I never thought I'd work for my best friend, but it's a good little gig. The hours are flexible, the people are friendly, and our coffee is also pretty damn good. I have to admit my boss is cool too.

"Morning!" Scarlett calls out as she strides into the café, pulling off her sunglasses with a smile. It looks like she's bounced back from Zack fairly well.

"Morning," I say as I stock the baked goods display case. "It's storming tomorrow."

Scarlett claps her hands in glee, her dangly bracelets clinking. "I have the best prize in mind."

"What's that?"

Scarlett taps around on her phone before

showing me a social media video of a couple enjoying a private beach and tanning next to a large pool. "A getaway!"

I could use a getaway soon.

"That's a great idea," I say with a nod of approval.

"Cocktails, white sand, and no screaming kids. I can't think of a better paradise," Scarlett says with a happy sigh as she wanders behind the counter to help me prepare the coffee bar.

"Careful, you're making me want to compete at game night," I warn her, sharing an amused look with her before turning toward the front door as a familiar man walks inside.

"Jake! Good morning!" Scarlett quips as she waves at him.

"Scarlett." Jake greets her before grinning politely at me. "Hailey."

"Medium flat white?" I ask him as I meet him by the register.

Jake chuckles and nods. From all the times he's come in, Scarlett and I have learned he has no girlfriend, but he has a hectic husky named Ash. "You got it."

I check him out before getting to work on his coffee, my hands moving automatically at this point.

"How would you react if you won a trip to a beach resort?" Scarlett asks him.

"I can't see anyone being mad about that. I know I'd enjoy it," Jake replies as he adjusts the collar of his button-down shirt. "Why? Am I your thousandth customer or something?"

I laugh a little as I pitch a quick look at him over my shoulder. "We're hosting a game night tomorrow. Players are divided into tables, and they have to play five board games. Whoever finishes all five first wins."

Jake raises his eyebrows in interest. "Oh yeah. I think I've heard about your game nights before. I'll see if a buddy of mine can come with me, and we'll give it a shot."

"That's the spirit!" Scarlett says.

I hand Jake his cup of coffee. "Have fun at the grind."

Jake laughs and tips his coffee cup toward me. "This will keep me going. You guys have a good day."

"See ya!" Scarlett quips before turning to me. "This game night is going to be one of our best yet. I can just feel it."

I think she's worked through most of her sadness and is seeing things in a brand-new, sparkly light, but I don't argue. I'm just glad she's feeling better. "Do you have any other games in mind? I feel we always have the same thing."

"Let me ask for a suggestion," Scarlett replies as another regular walks in. Before eight o'clock, we typically get the same crowd of regulars who grab a cup of coffee before heading to work. "Good morning, Mrs. Braison! I have a question for you."

Mrs. Braison works at First Bank just a few blocks from here. She always wears a blazer and skirt set to work, and even if I'm not facing the door, I can tell it's her by the clicking and thumping of her heels on the floor. "What's that, dear? And just my usual with an apple cinnamon muffin, Hailey. Thank you."

"Yes, ma'am," I say before getting to work on her cappuccino.

"What's your favorite board game?" Scarlett asks as she slips on a pair of disposable gloves before grabbing Mrs. Braison's muffin from the baked goods case. She places the muffin in our small oven, hitting the thirty-second button to warm it up.

Mrs. Braison lets out a soft laugh. "Oh dear. I haven't played one in so long. I believe my favorite was Monopoly."

"I love a good game of Monopoly," Scarlett replies with a beaming smile. She grabs the muffin out of the oven and rings Mrs. Braison up as I finish putting the lid on her coffee cup. "We're hosting a game night tomorrow. The winning table gets a resort trip!"

"I've been meaning to work on my tan," Mrs. Braison says as she takes her muffin and coffee. She flashes us a smile before heading out of the café.

"I want to be like her when I'm older." Scarlett sighs wistfully, coaxing a laugh out of me. "I'm going to pick out the other games. Hold down the fort!"

I playfully salute before she disappears into the back, leaving me alone at the front. Tomorrow night is going to be a night to remember for sure. Hopefully, for good reasons.

CHAPTER TWENTY THREE

The rain starts early on Friday, beginning in the morning with a drizzle and increasing with each passing hour.

"Hopefully, it doesn't flood," I say as Scarlett and I stand near the front door to watch the light downpour through the glass.

Scarlett drops her head back with a groan. "Don't speak it into existence."

I smirk at her and cross my arms, watching the last customer we served hurry out to his car. It's often quiet a little bit after lunchtime, but things will pick up the closer it gets to six o'clock when game night starts. I start to step away to go wipe down the tables when Scarlett suddenly grabs my arm.

"Is that Eric?"

I whip back around and narrow my eyes to see through the rain, but I don't have to look long before seeing Eric hurry from his car to the front of the café. He bursts inside with a brown paper bag in his hand and his cast hidden beneath his rain jacket. My jaw drops. "What are you doing here? You're supposed to be resting!"

Eric cracks a grin and kisses me on the cheek. "I've healed enough to drive and wanted to surprise you with lunch. Don't worry. I got something for you too, Scarlett."

Awe gleams in my eyes as a happy ache fills my chest. He constantly reminds me why we're getting married soon, and even if there is stress revolving around the wedding, I can't wait for it. "Thank you."

"You're the best," Scarlett adds as she places her hands over her heart. "I hope you're coming to game night."

"I'll be there for support," Eric promises as we walk to a nearby table to unpack two grilled chicken sandwiches with sides. He holds his arm close to him, doing the most he can to help out with one hand.

"They still haven't found the asshole who hit you?" Scarlett asks as she pokes around at the grapes and oranges in her fruit cup.

Eric shakes his head. "I check in with the head detective every day, but they haven't found anything yet. They may never find anything."

"That's just not right," Scarlett replies as her eyes narrow. "You could've gotten killed!"

I fully agree, but I can also tell Eric is tired of constantly checking and worrying about it. It's terrible he got hurt, but I'm just happy he's still alive when it could've been so much worse.

"I just have to move forward," Eric replies with a shrug before bumping his shoulder against mine with a grin. "But at least I'm still here to annoy you until the end of time."

I laugh and lean closer to press a brief kiss against his lips, unable to resist that magnetic pull I've felt lingering between us since day one.

"Ew. I love you guys," Scarlett says as she smiles at us.

I put my arm around Scarlett's shoulders, pulling her flush against my side as we all huddle together around the table. They're two of the most important people in my life, and I can't imagine getting through the days without them. "And we love you."

We all share a warm look until a customer hurries into the store to escape the rain, water droplets plummeting off his umbrella as he closes it. Eric places his hand on my lower back as he leans closer to me. "I should get going anyway. I'm going to run a few errands and then come back here in time for game night."

I nod and hug him goodbye, my lips hovering near his ear. "Thank you for lunch. I'll be sure to pay you back for it."

Eric smiles and shakes his head. "I got it

covered. It wasn't that much."

I lift an eyebrow at him as a playful smile crosses my lips. "I wasn't going to pay you back that way."

Realization sparks in Eric's eyes, coaxing him to chuckle and nod. "Well, I certainly won't say no to whatever you have in mind."

I give him a nudge toward the door before anything escalates, but the moment he leaves, I immediately yearn for him to come back. Given it's a little past two, it won't be long before he does.

"Hailey!"

"Coming!" I say before grabbing our trash and heading behind the counter to get back to work.

I make a handful of lattes and sell the rest of our scones before I shift to game night duty, which includes spacing out tables for teams to play at, setting up the first board game, and making sure our refreshment cooler is stocked with water, energy drinks, fruit juices, and sodas. By the time I'm done rushing all over the place, my feet ache, and people are starting to pour in.

"Welcome! Feel free to drape your raincoats over the backs of those chairs lined up along the wall. Drinks and snacks are available for purchase. In ten minutes, I'll explain the rules and the prize, and we'll get started!" Scarlett announces as she beckons all of our drenched guests inside.

I walk closer to the front door to peer through the glass, my eyes widening at how much the wind and rain have picked up. The trees outside almost look like they're swaying because they're being battered so much by the wind, and the parking lot has already started to mildly flood. We've got a long, wet night ahead of us, but that makes for the best game nights.

By the time Eric arrives, the teams are divided up between five tables, and Scarlett is midway through the rules and having to raise her voice above the loud drone of rain and the occasional rumble of thunder. The first game is Life, which most people seem to know how to play, so I only have to assist a few newbies before stepping off to the side.

"Remember, no tampering with your scoreboards! Hailey and I will mark off the games you completed. The first table to ring the bell twice and finish all five games is the winner!" Scarlett calls out. She waits a few seconds for everyone to get ready before throwing her hand up. "And go!"

"Board games are competitive enough. Only Scarlett can make it as daunting as getting through the playoffs," Eric tells me as we stand by the ordering counter together.

I crack a smile and nod. "Oh yeah. These people will nearly kill each other for a chance at a resort stay."

I can't say I blame them.

Eric glances toward the front of the café at the sound of lightning crackling in the sky nearby. "The storm is getting worse."

We must be the only ones who've noticed because everyone else is so engrossed in their games they're not even bothering to acknowledge the uptick in lightning cracks and thunder rumblings coming from right outside.

"Maybe I should check—"

Before I can even finish my sentence, a loud snap of lightning flashes right outside, and the lights go out in an instant. Gasps and shocked laughs echo throughout the café as everyone glances at each other in the near-total darkness.

"Just remain seated! We'll have to use phone flashlights until we find some candles," Scarlett announces before shining her flashlight in front of her as she approaches me. "Mother Nature is ruining my vibe. Can you check the back room for candles?"

"Of course," I reply as more phone lights start to illuminate the café as flashes of lightning continue to dance outside.

"I'll help," Eric says.

I lead him to the back room where we keep things in storage, my hand feeling along the wall for the light switch. "It should be right here."

I shuffle more to the right before my foot strikes something solid, making me stumble.

Like he has a sixth sense, Eric reaches out with his good arm and wraps it around me, anchoring my body against his. "You okay?"

I catch my breath and nod, my heart pounding from the sudden scare. "Yeah, thanks to you."

Eric moves closer to me, his back pressing flush against my chest. "You know I always have your back."

The feeling of his hand on my hip sends a wave of warmth rolling through my body, prompting me to turn around. I can barely make out any features of his face, but I can *feel* him there. "Now's my chance to thank you for earlier."

I can't see him, but I can just sense he's smiling. The hand on my hip moves to the small of my back as I lift on my toes to press my lips against his. My hands move up his chest and over his upper arms, feeling the grooves of muscle beneath his shirt from his work.

Eric lightly drags his teeth along my bottom lip in a teasing bite, making my next exhale come out shakily. He grins before kissing me again, our lips brushing and meeting in perfect rhythm.

Heat works its way through me as our kiss deepens, and the rest of the world falls away for just a few minutes before we have to return to reality. Right now, it's just me and him, and there's nothing more comforting than the thought of that.

Especially with what's lurking around the corner.

CHAPTER TWENTY FOUR

Warm water envelops me as I sink into my bathtub, a relieved sigh drifting from me as I get settled. My neck rests against the tub's edge, my eyes shifting to the ceiling. I definitely needed this.

The wedding is this week! My stomach flip-flops between excitement and nervousness as my brain races through every detail, making sure I haven't forgotten anything. According to everyone helping me with the preparations, everything is on track and ready for the ceremony and reception. That means my only job is to relax and not age ten years in the next few days.

My teeth press into my bottom lip as I chew on the soft tissue absentmindedly, my thoughts shifting to my guests. Most people who we invited have confirmed they're coming, and I even got a sincere apology from Eric's mom about the weight comment. Of course, it was awkward hearing her stumble through an overexplained apology. We've yet to hear from her, unsure if she's even coming to the wedding now. So I've had to move forward. I'm sure it upsets Eric.

I could've lingered on it more and made a bigger deal about it, but when I look at my family versus Eric's family, it's clear why more of his family will be there than mine. My father's side has never made me feel truly welcome, and despite my attempts at smoothing things over between my father and me and our shared relatives, there will always be bad blood. That means my side of the aisle is emptier.

What's even worse is the fact Ray isn't here to witness my marriage. When my own father screwed up every chance to be a parent to me, Ray stepped up and showed me what a real dad is supposed to act like. Holding the wedding on his birthday is my one way of feeling closer to him with him being gone.

My eyes sting at the thought, but I blink the sensation away and drag in a deep breath to try to relax myself. Despite my attempts to fight it, my mind jolts back to my father and his sudden death. Getting that letter shook me to my core.

That's how he wanted to let me know about his death? A letter? I guess that's better than getting a text or something, but I expected more than that. I thought I'd get a deeper explanation and maybe a little bit of closure.

Instead, I wasn't invited to the funeral, and

I received a gutting explanation from my uncle about how I would've caused more stress and drama if I had shown up. I didn't have a great relationship with my father in the slightest, but I didn't expect to be outcasted by that side of my family in such a confusing, emotional time. After that, I received no updates at all.

My eyes narrow as I ponder on that some more. I thought maybe someone would at least send me a picture or tell me how it went, but all I heard was radio silence. That's just… weird, but I suppose I can chalk it up to a lack of care for me.

A curious tug on my mind weakens me, and I end up leaning out of the tub to dry off my hands and grab my phone. Typically, obituaries are listed in the local newspaper, so I start by searching my father's name, expecting to see a small article that shares a little bit about his life and family.

But there's nothing.

Maybe they didn't have a public obituary posted for privacy reasons, but where is the one place older people don't care about preserving their privacy?

I open up my Facebook app and scroll through my aunts' profiles, trying to find photos or posts about the funeral or even about their brother passing. If they can post about the server who was rude to them or share a picture of the cake they made, they can share their thoughts about a family death.

I scroll and scroll, but there's nothing. I can argue that their brother's death is too difficult to post about, but they're all attention seekers. They wouldn't dare miss out on the chance to gain sympathy points from other people.

So why didn't they post? Why haven't they said anything about him since a week before his death?

There must be a reason they're being so private. Was his death suspicious or shameful? Are they keeping it hush-hush so the rest of the family doesn't feel embarrassed?

As twisted as that scenario is, I don't believe my father's side of the family is above that.

None of my scenarios sate my curiosity and suspicions, though. I want to know why my dad's death isn't public in any way, especially since he wasn't the hermit type. He had friends and chatted about his problems on Facebook for people to see. Total privacy is an odd request for someone on that side of the family.

I suppose I can ask my aunts and uncle about it. I have no idea what kind of answer to expect, but if I want an answer at all, I think I need to catch them off guard. Every Monday night, my dad's siblings eat dinner together at Aunt Jamie's house. They started doing that when their parents were alive and continued the tradition, even as people started to pass away.

Even though it makes my stomach churn, I have to stoop to that level if I want answers. Before I move on to the next part of my life, I need to wrap up some loose ends from this part.

It starts and ends with my father, and I'm dying to move forward at last without looking back.

A sense of wariness looms over my head like a dark cloud as I approach Aunt Jamie's front door, the wooden steps of her porch lightly creaking beneath me. Maybe I shouldn't be doing this. Is this crazy?

"Come on," I mutter beneath my breath. If I don't do this, the curiosity will drive me mad, and I need to start relaxing as the wedding gets closer.

I knock on the white wooden door and step back, hearing muffled noises inside for a minute before the door finally cracks open. I lean to the side a little to see Aunt Jamie peering through the small gap with a surprised look on her face.

"Oh, Hailey. We weren't expecting you," Aunt Jamie says as she pulls the door open all the way. She glances behind her before looking back at me. "We were just finishing up dinner."

"Mind if I come in? Sorry to bother you," I ask with a hopeful look. I just need to ask a few questions to get this weight off my chest.

Aunt Jamie doesn't move at first, but she eventually nods and steps to the side so I can walk inside. The smell of pot roast lingers in her house as I follow her to the dining room, where Aunt Lisa and Uncle Bryan are eating dinner and chatting. They fall silent at the sight of me.

"Hey, kiddo. It's been a while," Uncle Bryan says as he stiffly nods to me.

"How are you?" Aunt Lisa asks as she abandons her silverware on her plate like she's lost her appetite.

The uneasiness in the air is impossible to ignore, and I feel like a total stranger when I sit down at the dining table. I'm family, but I still don't feel totally welcome here. "I'm doing fine. It's been a while since I've seen you all, so I just wanted to check in."

"We've been doing fine. I see a ring on your finger. Are you getting married soon?" Aunt Jamie asks as she takes a seat next to her sister.

Oh yeah. This is awkward. I didn't invite them to the wedding, but they didn't even invite me to my father's funeral. "This Saturday."

"Oh, how wonderful," Aunt Jamie replies with a smile that feels forced.

I can't take this awkward wedding talk. I'm here to do some investigative work without letting them know I think something suspicious is going on. "Are you all hanging in okay after... his death?"

I can't even say his name or call him my father out loud in front of them.

They all share a brief look as if they're surprised I asked.

"We're hanging on," Uncle Bryan replies, coaxing nods from the others. "About the funeral..."

I shake my head. "It's fine about me not coming. I guess I just feel a lack of closure, though."

"It was a nice, small ceremony," Aunt Lisa says, silence following her words.

That's it? They're either purposely keeping details from me or not caring enough to share them with me. "I figured it was small since no obituary was posted."

Uncle Bryan shrugs. "I don't think he'd care for that. I think we were all so shocked and heartbroken over his death that we didn't really care to put that on display for everyone in town to see."

The longer I stay here, the sillier I feel for even showing up. Why do I even really care? My father and I were always at odds, even when we tried to settle things. I'll never be close to his family, and they obviously don't want to share anything with me because they know of our complicated relationship.

I'm wasting my time by getting paranoid over every little thing. "Yeah, I guess you guys would know what he wanted best."

"Is there something specific you want to talk about?" Aunt Jamie asks as she lifts an eyebrow at me.

I shake my head and take a step back. "No, I just wanted to swing by. I'll let you get back to dinner. Sorry."

Before they can say anything else, I turn and walk out of the house with a burning face. I think I'm letting the wedding jitters drive me crazy and create problems where they don't even exist.

All I have to do is hold it together for a few more days. Hopefully, I can at least pull that off without coming apart at the seams.

CHAPTER TWENTY FIVE

Today is the day.

After months of planning, stressing, and waiting, I'm finally getting married to the love of my life. I'm moving to the next chapter of my life and shedding the heaviest, darkest parts of my past. Hopefully.

When I think about my future with Eric, I see blinding hope and a love that'll never fizzle out. With those things, we can build the life we want. One of peace and happiness.

All I want is to share that kind of life with him, and it's so close I can feel it teasing my fingertips.

"Oh, you look beautiful!"

I turn away from the standing mirror in front of me to see Scarlett stepping into the dressing room in her burgundy bridesmaid dress. From my pinned-up hair to my white ball gown with lace sleeves, I gesture to myself, a nervous look forming on my face. "Does everything look okay?"

Scarlett shoots me a pointed look as she crosses over to me. "Don't get caught up in your own head. Everything looks perfect."

I take a deep breath and nod, trusting her judgment and the fact she'll be honest with me no matter what. "How's everything out there?"

"Everyone is ready for you," Scarlett replies with a warm smile. "Are you ready?"

"I'm ready to marry him. Not so ready for all the eyes on me," I admit with a soft, nervous laugh. My hands threaten to shake as I adjust my sleeves with a rapidly beating heart.

"Both of you deserve all this attention on your special day," Scarlett says as she gives the bottom of my dress a light fluff. She pauses for a moment before speaking. "Are you still going to walk down the aisle by yourself?"

Ray should've been walking me down the aisle, but it's just me today. I believe he's here in spirit, though. Even if I feel like I'm about to pass out, a warm, comforting atmosphere in the air still feels like him. "Yes, and it's okay. Eric will be right down the aisle waiting for me."

"He's going to flip when he sees how gorgeous you look!" Scarlett says as she claps her hands, unable to contain her excitement.

I can't wait to see him. To feel him slip that ring on my finger. To feel his lips on mine after we share our vows. I'm ready for all of that. "It's time?"

Scarlett smiles and nods. "It's time."

I take one more deep breath before nodding, letting Scarlett lead me out of the dressing room and toward the main area where the ceremony is being held. My flat shoes lightly tap against the flooring as she hurries ahead of me to give a warning to whoever needs one.

I take in a deep breath. It's time to begin.

I stop in front of wooden double doors, my heart threatening to burst right out of my chest as I hear "Canon in D" start playing inside. A few moments later, the doors swing open, revealing the ceremony room where Eric, Scarlett, the officiant, and Eric's best man Jackson, who he also works with in construction, are waiting on a slightly elevated platform. The wooden benches are split on either side of the aisle, and everyone is standing and smiling at me from either side as I take my first few steps down the aisle.

I tighten my grip on my bouquet of burgundy peony flowers. My stomach twists, threatening to nauseate me until my eyes fall upon Eric as he stares at me in awe and shock. His expression lifts my worries like a disappearing fog, and I'm struck by a wave of emotion that saps my breath.

There's the man I'm marrying in his black

suit with a matching burgundy boutonniere. We've been waiting for this for so long, and it's finally time. For a few seconds, everything feels perfect! Until I hear my name shouted from behind me.

"Hailey, wait!"

I spin around just as my father bursts through the open doors in a white dress shirt and black slacks, my head immediately feeling light at the sight of him. "You... I... I thought you were dead!"

My father comes to a stop and catches his breath. He almost looks crazed with his wide eyes and the sweat brimming his forehead. "Did you really think you could get married without your own father walking you down the aisle?"

I flinch a little when I hear the obvious sneer in his voice, being taken back to all those times when he demeaned me. Put me down. Shamed me. And he's doing that now at my wedding!

My face hardens as I glare at him, anger burning within me and growing hotter and hotter. "You lied to me! Your brother and sisters lied to me! You sent me a letter saying you were dead! Why?"

"Were you sad when you got that letter? Did you care?" my father asks as he approaches me with narrowed eyes.

I step back before bumping into something

solid. I look over my shoulder to see Eric behind me with a stern expression on his face as he glares at my father. With his presence nearby, I'm hit with a surge of strength to face my father again. "I felt free. Free from you and your constant abuse!"

My father tips his head back and laughs. "You were always one for dramatics, Hailey. You really think you can so easily cut me out of your life?"

"You need to leave!" my mom's voice cries out from behind me.

After that, there's a swarm of voices, shouts and yells being exchanged all around me. I can barely even hear myself think! I reach out for Eric's good arm to steady myself, my heart threatening to leap out of my chest when my father takes a big step closer to me to the point where I can feel his breath on my face.

"You don't deserve happiness after how you've treated your own dad. You deserve nothing!" he hisses.

"Someone call the cops!" Eric shouts as he pulls me behind him, warning my father not to get a centimeter closer.

I remain hidden behind Eric as others form a wall between my father and me, keeping him contained until I hear sirens outside the building. Eric ushers me out of sight as I try to catch my breath and keep tears from falling. "He ruined it. He ruined everything."

Eric helps me sit down in the dressing room, his hand caressing my cheek. "No, he didn't. It's okay. The police have him."

I sniffle and shake my head. "We can't have the wedding today! And I wanted it to be today for Ray."

Eric frowns and presses his forehead against mine. "I know. I'm sorry. But any day we have the wedding will be special to Ray. It'll still be in honor of him."

"I just don't understand my dad. I just want to know what I've done to deserve every awful word he's thrown my way," I say before swallowing hard.

"Forget about him. I'll talk to the venue and see if they have an opening for next week, and we'll have the wedding without worrying about him," Eric replies as he holds my gaze.

I need answers. I need something. Some sort of closure. Even when he faked his death, I needed closure. "I'm going to the jail to visit him."

"What?" Eric asks, surprised by my switch in attitude.

"I want answers. He can't go away if he's trapped in a cell," I tell him before getting to my feet. My hands grab his upper arms. "Please. I'm sorry, but I don't think I can stomach picking up today's broken pieces, but I can confront him for breaking everything."

Eric nods after a moment and offers me a gentle smile. "It can all be fixed, and you can get the answers you need. I'll take care of the wedding stuff. You go talk to your dad."

My heart skips as I give him a grateful look, unable to even think of the best words to say. There are three words that pretty much express how I feel, though. "I love you."

"I love you," Eric replies and leans down to peck me on the lips. We share a small smile before he pulls away. "I'll find Scarlett so she can help you out of your dress."

At a loss for words, I merely nod and watch him go, listening to the heavy thud of my heartbeat. I'm operating off pure adrenaline and sheer will at this point because if I stop and think too long about how my wedding has fallen apart, I'll break down. I have to keep going.

I have to end things.

By the time I arrive at the jail, I get a text from Eric saying he talked to the venue and our new wedding date is next Friday. I'm just glad he was able to get a date so soon, and I hope nothing happens to screw that one up. The venue can only throw us a bone so much.

I text him back before heading into the

building and talking to the clerk at the front desk. As I'm led back toward the cells, my stomach twists and flips, nauseating me with every step I take. A part of me wants to flee, but I keep moving until I see him past the bars.

A smirk crosses my father's face as he wanders over to the bars and wraps his fingers around them. "Came to bail me out?"

For a second, my ears ring, and I feel like a scared little girl getting yelled at and chastised, but I ground myself to reality and remind myself I've grown up. I have the choice to cut him out of my life for good this time, but I need to ask a few questions first. "What did I do to make you hate me? Would you rather have had a son? Did I break your television in the middle of a game or something?"

My father chuckles and tilts his head at me. "Someone sounds a little insecure."

A jolt of anger hits me as I step closer. "You made me that way! You criticized every move I made, and we fought over everything! Why?"

"Some people just don't get along," my father says in a snide manner.

I ball my hands up into fists, fighting back frustrated tears. After all he's done today, can't he answer a single question? "Why did you ruin my wedding?"

"No bride should walk down the aisle without her father," my father replies as his icy gaze lands on mine. "I'm not sorry."

His words knock the breath out of me, and in the silence that follows, I realize he'll never answer my questions. He'll never grant me closure. He'll never explain or apologize for what he's done to me.

"Then I'm not sorry for cutting you out of my life for good," I say as my face hardens. "You'll be going to court for faking your death and harassing me, and the only people you'll have by your side are your siblings. I'll be sure to kindly text them and tell them they're being cut out of my life too because I know they helped you."

My father glares at me, but before he can even open his mouth to talk to me, I whirl around and storm out of the jail.

When I get in my car, I finally let the tears fall.

CHAPTER TWENTY SIX

I never expected I would need multiple therapy sessions days before my wedding, but here I am.

I mess with a lock of my hair as I sit on the same couch I always sit on during my sessions with Dr. Kale, who glances over my file in a chair across from me. "Thank you again for seeing me so much this week. This'll be my last time, at least for a while."

"Your wedding is in three days," Dr. Kale replies as she passes me a warm smile.

"I'm terrified something bad is going to happen again. That we'll just never get married because bad things will keep happening," I admit before swallowing hard as a surge of fear rushes through me.

"Specifically, because of your father?" Dr. Kale asks.

I nod. "All I wanted was closure from him, and he couldn't even give me that after ruining my wedding."

"You may have to create closure for yourself," Dr. Kale says.

"How do I do that?" I ask, aching for a way to put all of this behind me.

"You have to accept the fact your father will never do anything to please you or make you feel at peace. For reasons we don't know, he's threatened by you. That causes him to lash out and try to drag you down below him," Dr. Kale explains.

That makes some sense. I don't know why he'd be threatened by me, but I certainly disturb his peace like he disrupts mine. "I'm just ready to move forward without him and all the pain he's brought me."

Dr. Kale smiles. "What steps have you taken to eliminate him from your life?"

"The first thing I did was tell my aunts and uncle that I don't want any contact from them. I know they helped him and lied right to my face when I asked about him," I say. I knew something suspicious was going on! "And I filed for a restraining order against my father."

"Those are great steps to take. No contact is a strong boundary to set," Dr. Kale tells me. "You should be proud of yourself for setting that boundary."

I'd like to see my dad try to ignore that restraining order because it'll land him right back in jail away from me. "I'm just... done. I'm getting to a point where I don't even care about getting answers from him. I'll be disappointed one way or another. He's like this infection in my life, and the best way to get rid of him is to cut him out completely."

"It sounds like you're stronger than you were at the beginning of this week," Dr. Kale says.

"I feel stronger," I tell her. Maybe part of it is defiance, but I don't feel restless and destroyed at the thought of not having answers. At this point, I never want to see my father again because he's just a force of destruction.

"You deserve to be happy, Hailey. You've put up your boundaries and let go. Now, enjoy your wedding and live your life," Dr. Kale encourages me.

A smile, one of relief and happiness, spreads across my face as the weight drops from my shoulders. She's right. I've set my boundaries and cast out the darkness in my life. If it tries to make a presence again, I have the best support team around me and the law to use as my shield.

"Thank you," I tell her, knowing I was a handful this week on such short notice.

"Thank you for advocating for yourself and coming to see me," Dr. Kale replies warmly.

After another profuse thank you and goodbye, I leave her office and go home to find

Eric getting off a phone call. A flicker of anxiety sparks in my mind. "Everything okay?"

Eric turns and grins. "Yep. I was just confirming everything with the last vendor. We're all set to get married this Friday, baby."

I release a sigh of relief and wind my arms around his neck, leaning against his firm body as he rests his hand on my hip. "I can't wait."

"How was your visit?" Eric asks after kissing the top of my head.

I smile against his chest, realizing I don't feel the same amount of stress about the wedding I did before. I feel... lighter. "It was good."

Eric caresses the back of my head and kisses my forehead. "I'm happy for you, and I'm so proud of you."

I tilt my head back to gaze up at him. "Thank you for sticking by me through this. Through everything."

Eric shakes his head. "You don't have to thank me for that. I love you. Of course, I will be by your side no matter what."

It still means the world to me, though. He's seen me at my best and my worst, and I was a wreck at the beginning of this week. He's helped keep me together, and Dr. Kale sealed up the remaining broken pieces. "I'm tired of not being married to you."

"Just a few more days, and you'll have

plenty of me," Eric replies with a cheeky grin.

I laugh and shake my head at him. "I can't wait."

Eric meets my gaze, a quiet, comfortable moment passing between us. Somehow, words and feelings are exchanged even in silence. I can feel them radiating between us as we stand together, healing from the past and turning to the future.

It's just within reach, and this time, we're going to make it.

CHAPTER TWENTY SEVEN

"ALL RIGHT, LET'S TRY THIS AGAIN."

Scarlett and I can't hold back the laughter that bursts from us as we once again stand outside the wooden double doors leading to the ceremony room. I place my hand on my stomach as it aches, my other hand fanning my eyes to keep my makeup from running.

"I'm sorry. That was a bit twisted," Scarlett says as she holds my arm, doing her best to contain her laughter.

"I wouldn't expect anything else from you," I tell her with an amused smile. Once we gather ourselves, I take a deep breath and look back at her. "Everything is going to be perfect."

Scarlett perks up at my confident words and nods. "Everything is going to be perfect. You're going to get married to the man of your dreams and run off into the sunset."

That sounds like the dream.

"I'm ready. I don't want to wait any longer,"

I say as I adjust the bottom of my dress, dying to get inside.

I'm not even nervous about all the eyes on me anymore. The worst has literally already happened, so things can only go up from here. I'm going to make it down that aisle by myself without tripping, and I'm not looking back.

Scarlett pouts in awe before giving me a careful hug. "I'm so happy for you."

"I'm glad you're here," I say.

She's been in my corner for so long. I need her here on this day. The happiest day of my life.

"I wouldn't miss it for the world," Scarlett tells me as she holds my upper arms. "As your best and only bridesmaid, it's my duty to be your beacon of stability during your ceremony and your hardest partier at your reception."

Another laugh breaks from me as my mind shifts to the reception after our ceremony. There will be plenty of dance music, incredible food, and a stocked bar for everyone to enjoy. It'll be a perfect way to end a perfect day. "I expect nothing less."

"Then let's get this show on the road!" Scarlett quips, shooting me one more smile before slipping inside.

The doors close again, and I'm alone in the hallway. But I don't feel alone. Everyone I love is in that room, and I believe that Ray is watching right now. He's part of this day just like everyone else, and he'll be with me when I walk down the aisle.

He's the only man who deserves to be by my side during that moment.

"Canon in D" starts playing inside, and I only have to impatiently shift on my feet for a few seconds before the doors swing open. I see the same setup as I did last time. Everyone stands and faces me, but the air is different. It's full of hope and relief.

There's no darkness on this day.

I walk between the rows of people, my gaze staying on Eric as he watches me with awe in his eyes. It's like he's seeing me for the first time. Like what happened before didn't occur.

What matters is that it won't happen again. I will never deal with the destructive force that is my father again, which means I'm free. I'm finally free to live my life without that looming darkness that has sucked so much happiness and light out of my life.

Today is a sunny day in more ways than one.

Warm smiles surround me as I pass by the front rows where his parents and my mom are seated, and when I reach Eric, the remaining worries I had about tripping and falling evaporate. I take his hands and smile at him, my heart pounding heavily. "I made it."

"You made it," Eric says with a chuckle.

I give his hands a squeeze, my eyes flickering past him briefly as Scarlett gives me a thumbs-up. I manage to withhold my laughter this time and merely smile before looking back up at Eric as his eyes sweep over me and my dress.

"You look beautiful," Eric says with awe in his voice.

"You look amazing," I reply, admiring the way his suit perfectly hugs his body. The splash of burgundy from the boutonniere ties it all together, and I'm struck by the fact I have such a handsome groom.

I did well. Really well.

"Ready?" Eric murmurs with soft, comforting eyes. The same ones that have encouraged me to open up and have brave conversations I thought I wouldn't ever share with anyone. The same ones that accompanied the words "I love you" so many times.

"Absolutely!" I say without a shred of hesitation before Eric and I turn to the officiant, who smiles at us.

"Welcome, everyone. We are gathered here today to witness and celebrate the marriage of Hailey Scott and Eric Carter," the officiant announces as he gestures to us. "Two souls meant as one will unite today, and now, they will pledge their everlasting love for one another for all to witness. Nothing is more powerful than love, and these two are proof of that."

I share a loving look with Eric as the officiant speaks, my heart fluttering wildly in my chest like trapped butterflies. We've come so far together. There have been obstacles and pitfalls along the way, but we've been there for each other every single time.

We haven't been stopped. We won't be stopped.

"Eric, do you take this woman to be your lawfully wedded wife, to have and to hold, in sickness and in health, for better or worse, for richer or poorer, from this day forward, as long as you both shall live?" the officiant asks him.

Without hesitation and with his radiant smile, Eric nods. "I do."

When the officiant turns to me and repeats the same words, the rest of the world falls away. It's the man I love and me. My best friend and my rock. The one I can always turn to.

Our future is finally in our grasp, and the past is behind us. The path ahead is clear and welcoming, and I'm excited for what comes next. I'm ready to create a life with him, that's everything we've ever wanted, and I'm ready for forever with him.

"I do."

ABOUT THE AUTHOR

Amy Rose was born and raised in Springfield, Illinois.

She has a deep love for romance, fantasy, dystopian, and action/adventure book genres.

Amy's writing journey began in the second grade when her teacher gave her a personal journal. Since then, writing has been a huge passion and something she will never stop doing.

Over the years, she faced many mental health and physical struggles from ADHD, Asperger's, Depression, Panic Disorder, and Chronic Pain, but she has never allowed the challengeds to stop her nor define who she is.

OTHER TITLES BY AMY ROSE

VANISHED DUOLOGY

Vanished

Vanished: The Quantum Chronicles

BREWING LOVE AND LATTES SERIES

That's What Love Is

That's What Love Becomes